Amy Cross is the author of more than 100 horror, paranormal, fantasy and thriller novels.

STRANGE LITTLE HORRORS

& OTHER STORIES

AMY CROSS

This edition
first published by Blackwych Books Ltd
United Kingdom, 2020

Copyright © 2020 Amy Cross

ISBN: 9798551769262

Also available in e-book format.

www.blackwychbooks.com

CONTENTS

STRANGE LITTLE HORRORS

& OTHER STORIES

STRANGE LITTLE HORRORS

"Have you ever watched your life drain away before your eyes?" Billie asked as she climbed out of the car and looked at the ramshackle old farmhouse. "Have you ever felt the exact moment when you start circling life's plughole?"

"It's amazing!" her little sister Janey yelled, racing around from the other side of the car and rushing over toward the building. "Are we really gonna live here? Are we?"

"I want to kill myself," Billie continued, rolling her eyes. "This is the worst move ever."

"And you're sure you're not exaggerating just a little?" Catherine asked, slamming the car door shut before putting a hand on her daughter's shoulder. "You're going to like it here, I promise. It'll just take some time to settle in, that's all."

Turning, Billie looked around and saw

nothing but fields of grass stretching away from the farmhouse in every direction. The only break from the monotony of the view was a faint smudge on the horizon, although even when she squinted Billie wasn't quite sure what she was seeing.

"Is that a scarecrow?" she whispered. "Like, an actual, real scarecrow?"

Not that it mattered, anyway; as far as Billie was concerned, moving to a remote farm in the middle of nowhere meant that her life was now officially over.

"Can you help me get the things inside?" Catherine asked. "I think your sister's too busy exploring."

"Why does *she* get to slack off?" Billie asked, watching for a moment as Janey ran to the small barn near the house. "It's totally not fair. Dad never used to let her get away with half the stuff she gets away with now."

"Help me unpack the car, please," Catherine said, with a hint of discomfort in her voice. "The sooner we do that, the sooner we can start making this place feel like home."

***

"I'm a ghost!" Janey yelled, running into the farmhouse's front room with a sheet over her head. "Look at me! Am I scary?"

"As a representative of your generation," Billie muttered, barely glancing up from her phone, "you're terrifying."

"That's enough from you," Catherine said, suddenly stepping into the doorway and blocking Janey's path, before pulling the sheet from over her head. "Have you brushed your teeth, like I asked?"

"Yes!" Janey announced proudly, displaying her teeth for her mother to see.

"And have you brushed your hair?"

"Maybe!" Janey added, with equal gusto.

"Go and brush your hair, young lady," Catherine said, steering her youngest daughter toward the hallway. "You'll be the first one to complain if it's a tangled mess in the morning."

Stepping back into the front room, Catherine stopped for a moment and put her hands over her face. She stood completely still, as if she was taking a few seconds to completely reset her mind.

"You okay?" Billie asked, briefly glancing at her.

"Just thinking of the million and one things we have to do tomorrow," Catherine replied, lowering her hands. "We emptied the trunk of the car, that's good, but the back seat is still piled high. Would you mind getting up a little early in the morning and helping me with that?"

"How early are we talking?"

"What if I make a really nice breakfast and

have it on the table for, say, seven?"

"Is that going to be a thing now?" Billie asked, making no effort to describe her lack of interest. "Family breakfasts?"

"You used to like it when your father did it."

"Yeah, but Dad's..." Bille caught herself just in time. There were times when she wanted to sound like a sullen teen, and times when she figured she should hold back a little. "I just don't see what we're doing here," she continued finally. "I get that we had to downsize, but this place is ridiculous. Do we have a plan, Mom, or is this just, like, a holding pattern until we come up with something better?"

"I'm going to finish sorting the beds out," Catherine said wearily, turning and heading to the stairs. "If your little sister comes back through, try to keep her from climbing up the walls."

"Like that's gonna work," Billie muttered under her breath, as she returned her gaze to her phone.

She tapped at the screen a few times, but still the page wouldn't load.

"And the internet still isn't working!" she called out. "There's no signal out here, so we need the internet to work or we're, like, completely cut off from the world! Is that what you want, Mom? Do you want us to be like settlers on some other planet and -"

Before she could finish, she heard a loud

bump coming from out on the porch. She turned and looked over at the windows, which only reflected the light from inside the room. Outside, darkness had fallen and for a moment Billie could only think about the vast fields of nothing that lay all around the farmhouse. She'd tried not to consider the possibility of serial killers or monsters or rural people being anywhere nearby, but she couldn't deny that the farmhouse had certain horror movie vibes that made her feel a little uncomfortable.

Once she was sure there was nothing out there, she looked back down at her phone.

Almost immediately, she heard the sound again, this time accompanied by a brief tapping sound. She looked over at the windows again, and then she got to her feet. She wanted to call out to her mother, but at the same time she didn't want to admit that she was scared, so instead she walked to the windows and peered out at the darkened porch.

She couldn't see anything, but then that didn't mean much. The porch was long, and anything could be hiding out there.

"If this is some rabid raccoon," she said with a sigh, as she unlocked the door and pulled it open, "I will officially scream."

Stepping out onto the porch, she felt an immediate brace of cold air. There was a light on the wall, but she had no idea where she might find a switch, so instead she had to look both ways along the dark porch and squint in an effort to make out any shapes. So far, so good, although she quickly realized that she felt as if she was being watched. She tried to put that down to nerves, but the sensation grew and finally she looked out at the fields of grass. Something was wrong, something on the edge of her perception seemed to have noticed something, even if her conscious mind hadn't quite gotten it all figured out just yet.

She made her way to the railing and looked out again, and after a moment she realized what was wrong.

The scarecrow was gone.

She was sure she was looking in the right direction, but even when she stood on tip-toes she found that the scarecrow seemed to have disappeared. There was enough moonlight for her to be able to see way out across the field, somehow the scarecrow was missing. She figured there was a chance it might have simply fallen over, or that it might have been removed by some busybody, although neither of those explanations felt particularly likely. The only alternative, she figured, was that she was mistaken, that the scarecrow had been off on the other side of the house, although she was sure that -

Suddenly hearing a scratching sound, she turned and looked along the porch again. The sound quickly stopped, but this time Billie was certain that there was definitely something nearby.

Something alive.

"Hello?" she said cautiously, before telling herself that she was being stupid. Most likely, there was some kind of rural critter on the porch. "Hey, whatever you are," she continued, "you might as well beat it."

She waited, and after a few seconds she realized she could hear something moving behind the old bench that the previous owners had left on the porch. She flinched slightly, before reminding herself that there was no reason to be scared of some dumb animal. Still, she couldn't deny that she felt a little nervous as she started making her way slowly toward the bench. She was ready for some kind of creature to come scuttling out at any moment, so she took a moment to carefully shut the door into the house before resuming her slow walk toward the bench.

"If you think we're gonna feed you," she continued, "you're seriously mistaken, okay? You might as well just give up and get, like, a thousand miles from here."

Reaching the end of the bench, she realized that the sound had stopped now. In her mind's eye, she couldn't help imagining some kind of huge rat, and she had to remind herself that there was no real reason to be scared. Sure, rats could bite, but she figured this one would run away as soon as it got the chance. Still, she wanted to play things safe, so she grabbed an old broom that was resting against the wall, disturbing a few spiders in the process.

"Gross," she muttered under her breath, as she got ready to move the bench out of the way. "Don't say I didn't warn you. If you put up a fight, I will end you."

With that, she pulled one end of the bench away from the wall. She braced for something to rush at her, but instead all she saw were some dead leaves and a few old metal poles. She looked out toward the edge of the porch, in case she was able to spot the rat running away, and then she sighed as she dragged the bench back into position and set the broom back down. She was already starting to think that perhaps she'd imagined things, that perhaps rural life was just going to involve a few weird noises now and again.

Feeling tired, she wandered back toward the door.

Suddenly, just as she reached out to pull the door open, she heard another scratching sound coming from over her shoulder. She froze, listening as the sound continued, and now she was starting to feel as if some type of vermin was playing games with her. She wanted to just go back inside and try to make the router work, but after a moment she figured she should at least try to get eyes on whatever creature was causing so much trouble.

That way, she and her mother would know what kind of trap to buy in the morning.

Turning, she saw nothing nearby, which made her feel -

"Boo!" a voice yelled, as something rushed at her from the left.

Startled, Billie turned and pulled the porch door open, but at the same time she took a step forward. She meant to hurry back inside, but her timing was a little off and so instead she succeeding simply in pulling the door straight against her face, and she let out a cry of pain as she felt her nose break.

***

"It was only a joke!" Janey sobbed again, sitting on the armchair in the front room. "I didn't mean it!"

"It's definitely broken," Catherine said as she continued to examine the bloodied mess in the center of Billie's face. "Honey, I'm going to have to get you to the emergency room."

"How bad is it?" Billie gasped, her voice sounding muffled as she held a cloth against her nose. "I can take it, Mom. Tell me. Is it going to be crooked for the rest of my life?"

"I'm sure it'll be fine," Catherine replied, getting to her feet, "but it really does need to be looked at right now."

"You little piece of shit!" Billie snapped, turning to her sister. "What the hell is wrong with you?"

"It was a joke!" Janey yelled, red-faced and angry. "I didn't know you were going to open the door into your own face! I only wanted to scare you!"

"I oughta break your nose in revenge," Billie replied with a scowl. "This isn't funny, Janey! It really hurts!"

"I'm sorry!" Janey bawled. "It was a joke!"

"Can you please just stop shouting?" Catherine asked, clearly flustered as she hurried into the kitchen. "I need my bag and my keys. The emergency room's about a forty-mile drive, it's late but they're open all night."

"Do we really have to go?" Billie asked.

"I'm afraid so," Catherine said, quickly returning with her things, before stopping for a moment. "Damn, the car's a mess, there's no room on the back seat."

"I didn't mean it!" Janey whimpered, rubbing her eyes as fresh tears ran down her face. "It's not my fault she overreacted! I only wanted to scare her, I didn't mean to hurt her!"

"Just stop talking for a moment," Catherine replied, "I'm not -"

"It's not fair!" Janey shouted, clenching her fists and pounding the arms of the chair. "Why am I in trouble when she's the one who opened the door into her own face? I was only -”

“Shut up!” Catherine screamed suddenly.

Shocked, Janey stared at her mother for a moment before starting to cry again.

“I didn't mean that,” Catherine continued, as she helped Billie up from the sofa. “Janey, I'm sorry, it's just that I really didn't need this tonight, okay? It's going to take at least an hour to get to the emergency room from here, and it might take a few hours for them to fix your sister's nose up. We're going to be out all night.”

“It's not my fault!” Janey whined.

“Then whose fault is it, you little brat?” Billie shouted.

“Both of you, stop!” Catherine said, and she started helping Billie toward the door. “It's okay, we'll get it all sorted. I'm going to have to clean the stuff off the back seat of the car first, though. Damn it, why didn't I do that earlier, when I had the chance?”

“I'm not to blame for this,” Janey grumbled, sniffing back more tears as she began to follow them out of the farmhouse. “Daddy would be on my side. He never would have let this happen in the first place. We wouldn't even have to be in this stupid place if he was still alive.”

“What did you say?” Catherine replied, turning to her.

"I said -"

"That's it, young lady!" Catherine continued, suddenly unable to control her anger. "Do you realize how much trouble you've caused tonight?"

"But -"

"I don't have time for any of this," Catherine added. "You know what, Janey? You're ten years old, and I think that's old enough for you to learn a lesson in personal responsibility. I'm going to drive your sister to the emergency room, and you're going to stay right here until we get back."

"By myself?" Janey replied, her eyes opening wide with shock.

"I hope you get eaten by coyotes," Billie mumbled.

"No-one's getting eaten by coyotes," Catherine said firmly. "I'm sorry, Janey, but you caused this situation and I don't have the time or the patience to clear out the back seat of the car so you can come with us. So you're going to have to stay here instead, and I hope you'll use the time to think about your actions and to realize that there are consequences that you might not like."

"But I didn't do anything wrong," Janey sobbed. "She's the one who ran into the stupid door. This isn't fair, I'm not -"

"Be quiet!" Catherine shouted, turning to her with genuine anger in her eyes. "You're old enough to hold the fort for a few hours. And if you get scared, well... I suppose you'll just have to learn a lesson from that, won't you?"

***

Standing all alone at the front door, staring out at the road that led away from the farmhouse, Janey watched as the light from the car finally disappeared into the distance. Until that moment, she'd been absolutely convinced that her mother would turn the car around and return for her. Now, she was finding it a little harder to cling to that hope.

"It's not my fault," she whimpered, with fresh tears filling her eyes. "I didn't make Billie run into that door. She's the one who was stupid and didn't look where she was going, why am I being punished?"

She waited, watching the horizon and hoping that the lights would reappear at any moment, but now she was really starting to worry that she was getting left behind. She told herself that her mother would never leave her alone for hours and hours in an unfamiliar house, she reminded herself that she was too young, but then she thought back to her mother's anger. Sure, Janey had made her angry before, and she knew her mother had been stressed after everything that had happened, but the anger had never really boiled over before.

Not until tonight.

"I'm sorry," she whined, still waiting to see the car return, still hoping that her mother could somehow hear her. "I didn't mean it. It was just a joke."

Finally, as a particularly cold gust of wind made her shiver slightly, Janey realized that no-one was coming back. Not for a few hours, at least, so shut the door and made her way back across the kitchen. She was trudging unhappily, feeling very sorry for herself, and when she reached the front room she stopped again as her sense of isolation really kicked in. She was sorry for playing a prank on her sister, but she was also mad that she was being punished way too much for something that she still felt was partly Billie's fault.

"Stupid door," she muttered under her breath, as she spotted the porch door that had caused all the trouble. "Why did you have to be so hard?"

She headed to the sofa and flopped down, and then she put her head in her hands and started crying again. After a few seconds, she felt an unstoppable wall of anger pushing through her body, and she started slamming her feet against the floor as she erupted into a full-blown tantrum. Her face was redder than ever, tears were streaming from her eyes, and a moment later she began to punch the cushions.

"It's not fair!" she screamed. "I didn't mean it! It was only a joke, I didn't mean to -"

Suddenly she heard a loud thud coming from out on the porch, and she froze. Staring at the window, with tears still trickling down her face, she saw only the lights of the room reflected in the glass, but a moment later she heard another thud, and then another, as if something heavy was slowly but surely making its way along the porch. For a brief flicker of a second, Janey began to wonder whether her mother might have miraculously returned to fetch her, but there had been no sound of the car pulling up and no sign of the lights.

Another thud rang out.

Whatever was out there on the porch, it sounds like it was carrying a heavy sack.

Staring at the window, Janey felt more and more as if she was being watched, and finally she scampered off the sofa and hurried to the light switch. After plunging the room into darkness, she looked back at the window, and now she could just about see outside. She could see the moonlit field beyond the property, and the silhouette of the porch's railing, and she inadvertently held her breath as she waited in case some kind of figure came into view.

Now, however, the thudding sound had stopped.

Once she realized she was holding her

breath, Janey took a few big gulps in an attempt to catch up, but she couldn't take her gaze away from the window. She felt as if something was definitely out there watching her, and she was starting to feel as if her mother had made a really big mistake by leaving her alone. After all, none of them knew the farmhouse very well, and Janey figured that there might be all sorts of monsters lurking out there in the darkness. Had her mother even checked the place out properly before racing off into the night with Billie? Had she abandoned her youngest daughter in a property she didn't even know properly?

Janey was starting to feel as if she was the unluckiest girl in the whole world.

And then, slowly, she turned and looked back through to the kitchen as she realized she could hear a scratching sound. At first, she wasn't sure exactly where the sound was coming from, but a moment later she let out a gasp of shock as she saw that the handle of the front door was slowly turning.

Panicking, Janey pulled back out of sight, just as she heard the door clicking open. Her mother had instructed her to make sure it was locked from the inside, but in her anger Janey had completely forgotten to do that, and now she heard a creaking sound as the door very slowly began to swing open. She told herself that there was still no reason to panic, that the sound was simply caused by a gust of wind that had caught the door, but a moment later she heard the handle bump against the wall, and she felt a current of cold air blowing through into the house as the field of grass rustled in the late night air.

Janey looked over at the door that led into the hallway. She desperately wanted to run upstairs and hide under her bed, but she knew that she might end up attracting attention. Her heart was racing, and she tried to convince herself that she was simply imagining things.

Suddenly she flinched and almost cried out, as she heard another thudding sound, this time coming from the kitchen. Something was definitely in there, and a moment later she heard a scraping sound, as if some kind of sack was being dragged across the floor.

Pulling back further, Janey kept her eyes fixed on the door to the kitchen. She didn't dare move a muscle, and she tried to tell herself that nothing really bad was happening. Sure, her mother had been mean to leave her alone, but deep down she was certain that she'd never have done that unless she was sure that everything was safe. No matter how bad things had been in the past, Janey's parents had always been there to look after her. Now her father was gone, but she trusted her mother and she felt certain that nothing *truly* bad could ever happen.

A moment later, she heard another thud, and this time she saw some kind of large cloth sack landing on the floor in the doorway, as if it had been thrown forward by some unseen hand. There was clearly something large and heavy in the sack, and after a couple of seconds Janey heard a faint gasping sound coming from the kitchen.

Panicking, she ran past the counter and dropped down behind one of the chairs, determined to hide herself away from whoever was about to come through. She forced herself to be brave, and as she leaned out to take a look she saw that the sack was being lifted off the floor. Sure enough, it was thrown fully through into the front room, and finally Janey saw a figure stepping into view.

She immediately pulled out of sight and squeezed herself into a tiny ball, desperately hoping that she wouldn't be noticed. She knew she hadn't made too much noise so far, and she was clinging to the hope that the intruder might not even know that anybody was home.

She waited, and sure enough she soon heard the sound of the sack getting dragged a little further across the floor. She couldn't be sure, but she thought that it might be heading toward the hallway, in which case she'd have a chance to run through the kitchen and get out of the farmhouse. All she had to do was wait a little longer and not make a noise.

Another thud hit the floor, and this time Janey was certain that it was moving away. She knew she couldn't breathe a sigh of relief just yet, but she figured that the intruder was most likely going to go upstairs and look for people to murder, which meant that she'd be able to sneak out. In fact, she was starting to think that she'd chosen the best possible hiding place, and that all she had to do was wait until she got her chance to escape.

"I'm so sorry for leaving you home alone!" she imagined her mother saying later. "That was so bad of me, Janey. I'll never do anything like that ever again!"

"It was all my fault," she knew Billie would add. "I'm so sorry I got you into trouble, Janey. Can you ever forgive me?"

She *would* forgive them, Janey decided, but only if they showed that they were really sorry. First, though, she was going to have to get out of the farmhouse, and she felt a little flicker of relief as she heard the sack hitting the floor in the hallway. That meant that the person was getting further away, and already Janey felt tempted to make a run for the door. She just wanted to hear one more thud, and then she'd be ready, so she shifted her position a little so that she'd be poised to run.

Just as she was almost ready, however, she pressed her left foot against a slightly loose board, causing a brief but very loud creaking sound.

She froze.

Had the intruder heard?

She told herself that everything would be alright, but now the farmhouse had fallen silent and she began to wonder whether she'd made a terrible mistake. She needed to hear the sack again, to know which way it was being dragged, but the intruder seemed to be taking a long time to make a decision.

Finally, she heard the dragging sound, but she couldn't quite tell whether it was going further away or coming closer. A moment later, the sack thudded down again, and Janey flinched as she realized that it had definitely come back into the room.

She looked again toward the doorway that led into the kitchen. She imagined herself racing through into the next room, ducking out of the way of someone who was trying to grab her, but she couldn't quite bring herself to make the move. She was still hoping that the intruder would go upstairs so that she'd have a better run. After a few seconds, however, she heard the dragging sound again, and then another bump as the sack was dropped down.

This time, the impact was so heavy and so close, Janey felt it vibrating through her feet from the floorboards.

She immediately began to get up and run to the door, but only for a fraction of a second. Just as she'd begun to tense her muscles, something in her heart made her hold back and she barely moved at all. Instead, she kept her eyes fixed on the open doorway and she tried to imagine the perfect run, the perfect way to get out of the house, and she told herself that she'd simply run and run and run along the road that lead away from the farmhouse, and that eventually she'd find her mother and sister, and that they'd save her and -

Flinching, she heard the dragging sound again, and a moment later one end of the heavy-looking sack dropped down against the floor just a few inches in front of her.

Blocking her way.

Realizing that she'd have to run the long way around, past the other end of the chair, Janey turned to get ready. This time, she was going to really do it, and she wasn't even going to look up at the intruder's face. She decided to count down from ten, and that she'd run as soon as she got to one, no matter what happened. She began to prepare herself, but she was already down to five and she was starting to think that she wasn't brave enough.

Now she was down to three.

Two.

One.

Scrambling to her feet, she began to run around the chair, only to freeze as soon as she saw the intruder. Looking up, she saw that his face was covered by some kind of old cloth, with holes for his dead, rotten eyes, and she felt her heart jolt as she realized she was face to face with a real live, walking scarecrow.

She screamed.

***

"Okay," the doctor said as she adjusted the light and then peered closer at Billie's nose, "that should do you for now. It's not too bad, but you'll have to come back in about a week so I can take another look at it."

"How does it feel?" Catherine asked. "Does it hurt?"

Sitting on the end of the bed, Billie stared at her reflection in the mirror and saw the huge bandage that covered her nose. The sight was so ridiculous, so extreme, that she had to admit that it had a comical side, even if that was somewhat eclipsed by the fact that it was painful, and by the fact that she'd never be able to appear in public again. Already, she couldn't help imagining that the bandage would eventually be removed, only to reveal a crooked nose that would make her look like some kind of witch.

"It is what it is," she said with a heavy sigh. "I guess I'm just going to have to get used to being hideous."

"I should go and sort out a few things at the desk," Catherine said, clearly stressed, as she headed out of the room. "I'll meet you out front."

Once the door was shut, the doctor focused for a few minutes on fixing the bandage properly. Billie, meanwhile, simply sat in silence and waited for the ordeal to be over. She glanced at the clock and saw that it was almost 3am thanks to the long wait outside, and she realized that she probably still wouldn't get to bed for another couple of hours. She was starting to feel exhausted, but the brightness of the examination room was keeping him awake.

"So I saw from your form that you're living at the Rutter farm," the doctor said eventually.

"Is that what it's called?"

"Out on Rutherford Road."

"Yeah, I think that's the one."

"So what's it like there?"

"We only moved in today," Billie admitted. "So far, I haven't seen much of it. I'm not sure there's much of it *to* see."

"That place has been empty for a long time."

"You can kinda tell."

"You know much about it?"

Billie hesitated, and for the first time she was starting to feel as if the doctor was trying to get to some particular point.

"What's to know?" she replied finally. "It's

an abandoned, rundown farm that we're somehow supposed to turn into our home over the next few years."

"But do you know anything about its past?"

"What, did some serial killer live there?" Billie asked. "I don't think we've actually checked the basement yet. Are there meat hooks down there?"

"Not as far as I know."

"We got it dirt cheap, though," Billie explained. "Mom was looking for somewhere that wouldn't cost much, and the state was auctioning that farm off. No-one else bid. It was almost as if they were going to pay us to take it on."

"It's a nice big farm," the doctor pointed out. "Huge, really. It's a real shame that it's been left empty for so long."

"So why *has* it been left empty?"

The doctor hesitated for a moment as she worked on the bandage. She seemed to be trying to work out exactly what to say next.

"There have always been stories about that place," she said after a few more seconds. "People who lived there apparently felt that there was a presence, something that couldn't quite be explained. Nothing big, nothing over-the-top, just strange little horrors that cropped up now and again. Anyone who stuck around for too long used to claim that they felt they were being..."

Billie waited for her to continue.

"They felt they were being *what*?" she asked cautiously. "Watched?"

"Apparently it was more than that. It was like they were being... teased."

"Teased?"

"I'm just telling you what people say. That something on that farm likes to tease whoever lives in the farmhouse. Not that anyone's lived there for, like, a century or so. I don't know exactly what happened to the last people, but I get the impression they were pretty much run off their land."

"That sounds like some kind of legend," Billie said.

"It does, doesn't it? And I'm sure that's all it is, but I swear the whole county knows about the Rutter farm. Some of the stories are crazier than others, but..." She paused, before finishing with the bandage and sitting back. "There. Done. Ignore all that crap I just came out with, it's just the usual crap you get around here."

Easing herself up, Billie touched the bandage on her nose for a moment, and then she turned and watched as the doctor began to make some notes.

"Go on, then," she said, figuring that she had to know a little more, "what does everyone say about that stupid farm?"

"All sorts of contradictory things," the

doctor muttered, as she ticked some boxes and then turned one of the forms over. "The main theme seems to be that there's something living there, something that gets off on tormenting anyone who lives in the house. It's not like some massive evil or anything like that, it's more some kind of... annoyance. Like a joker."

"Seriously?" Billie paused for a moment. "Sorry, I've lived in the city my whole life, we don't really have stories like that in the city."

"That's probably very wise," the doctor said. "Leave all the creepy rural crap alone, it'll only end up driving you round the twist." She tore the page from the notepad and held it out to her. "Now take two of these, once a day, for a week, and come back to see me once you're out."

***

"I can't believe how long that took," Catherine said as she eased the car along the bumpy road that led back to the farmhouse. "I should never have left Janey alone for so long."

"She'll be fine," Billie replied, watching the patch of brightness on the horizon. "The sun's coming up, anyway. The little squirt'll be okay. If anything, it might have done her some good to get a little scared."

"It *was* an accident," Catherine pointed out.

"Remember that. She was being dumb, but she never meant to actually hurt you."

"I know," Billie muttered, as the car came to a halt outside the farmhouse. "She's just such a -"

Stopping suddenly, she couldn't help but notice that the front door was wide open. She told herself not to worry, but then she saw that there seemed to be no lights on inside the house. Even though she figured she was probably overreacting, Billie couldn't shake the feeling that the house somehow looked empty. As she climbed out of the car, she looked out for any hint that Janey was inside. She couldn't put her finger on any one particular problem, but something about the house just felt wrong.

"I can barely keep my eyes open," Catherine said as she made her way around from the other side of the car. "There's no point going to bed, though. How about I start making us a really early breakfast, and then we can get to work?"

She made her way toward the house, and then she stopped at the open door and turned back to Billie.

"Does that sound good?"

"Sure," Billie replied, trying to shake her sense of fear, and then watching as her mother headed inside. "Yeah, let's all have some big happy family breakfast, and then we can start getting this place into some kind of decent shape."

Still trying to shake the sense that something was wrong, Billie waited outside. More than anything, she wanted her little sister to come running out, to maybe play another prank, but deep down she was struck by a terrible conviction that something bad had happened to Janey. With each passing second, she tried to convince herself that she was just letting her imagination run wild, that perhaps she'd let that stupid doctor's warning get into her head, but some kind of fear was bubbling in the pit of her stomach and she just couldn't seem to push it away, no matter how hard she tried. The only solution, she knew, was for Janey to appear and prove that she was very much still alive.

As her anxiety grew, Billie began to clench and unclench her fists.

Suddenly Catherine stepped back into the doorway.

"That's odd," she said, looking around at the yard, "I can't find Janey."

Billie felt an instant tightening of the fear in her chest.

"Have you looked upstairs?" she asked, trying to stay calm.

"If she's trying to punish us for leaving her alone last night," Catherine replied, "then I am just about out of patience." She sighed, before stepping out of the farmhouse and putting her hands around her mouth. "Janey!" she yelled. "We're home! Do you want some pancakes?"

They both stood and listened for an answer. Billie didn't want to let her mother know how much she was panicking, and she still clung to the hope that there was nothing to worry about. She looked around for a moment, and then she turned back to her mother, waiting for a spot of reassurance.

"That kid," Catherine said with a sigh. "Okay, we have to find her. I swear, this is the last thing I need right now."

"I'm sure she's totally fine," Billie replied, although she could hear the sense of doubt in her own voice. "She's ten years old, she's just being a moron."

"I'm going to take a look in that barn or outbuilding or whatever the hell it is," Catherine said, turning and heading that way.

"I'll..."

Billie paused for a moment, and then – looking over her shoulder – she realized she could just about make out the scarecrow in the distance. It was the same scarecrow she'd spotted the day before, the same scarecrow that she'd then been unable to see from the porch. She glanced at the house, and she felt a sliver of concern as she realized that she should have been able to see it all along, over the low grass. She tried for a moment to figure out what might have gotten in the way, and then she looked back at her mother.

"I'm going to take a look over this way!" she called out. "Just in case!"

"If you find her, drag her back by her ear!"

Once Catherine was in the barn, Billie set off along the road. As her footsteps trudged against the dusty ground, she told herself that the most likely outcome was another 'surprise'. She was expecting Janey to leap out at any moment, and she was ready for that, and she began to rehearse the speech she was going to give her sister. She didn't want to be the responsible older one, not at the tender age of just fifteen, but at the same time she felt that she had a duty to remind Janey that their mother was having a hard time. She figured she'd also play the sympathy card a little and remind Janey about her broken nose.

After a few minutes, she had to head off the road and start picking her way through the grass. This slowed her down a little, but at least she was getting closer to the scarecrow, which she could now see was a rather scrappy thing attached to an old wooden post. Billie had never really thought much about scarecrows before, but she had to admit that this particular specimen was somewhat disturbing. When she finally stopped directly in front of the damn thing and looked up at its face, she scrunched her nose up as she saw the tattered cloth with two ripped eye holes and a slit for a mouth.

"Nice," she muttered, before looking around. "So, have you seen an annoying little kid anywhere around here? About four and a half feet tall, tends to get on everyone's nerves?"

She waited for a moment, before looking back up at the scarecrow.

"I noticed you were out and about last night, by the way," she continued. "Just so you know, I'm really not in the market for some kind of -"

Stopping suddenly, she realized she could hear a very faint sobbing sound coming from somewhere nearby. She turned and looked around, while telling herself that the sound had to be something else, but she was quickly coming to realize that someone seemed to be upset. The grass was fairly long, but finally she spotted a shape shuddering in the field, about twenty feet away.

"Janey?" she whispered, before hurrying off to take a closer look. "Janey, is that you?"

As she reached the shape, she saw that it was something inside a large cloth sack. There were holes in the sack, the material of which was stained dark red in places, and after a moment Billie realized she could smell a foul stench. The sobbing sound was coming from inside the sack, but Billie told herself that he had to be wrong, that this couldn't be her sister.

"Janey?" she said cautiously, before dropping to her knees.

She reached out to open the sack, but then she hesitated, unable to bring herself to take a look.

"Janey, that's not you, is it?" she continued, just as fresh blood dribbled from one of the sack's many holes. "What the hell..."

She swallowed hard, and then she forced herself to pull back the open end of the sack. Her hand was trembling, and a moment later she pulled back in shock as she saw the bloodied, shuddering mass of flesh that was all that remained of her little sister. For a few seconds, staring at the sack, she felt as if her brain had frozen, as if some inner circuit breaker had been triggered in a last desperate attempt to keep herself from understanding the true horror of what she was seeing. At the same time, a wave of anguish was rushing through her mind, ready to break through at any second as tears began to fill her eyes.

Suddenly she heard a crackling sound, and she turned to see that the scarecrow on the post was shaking wildly, almost as if it was laughing.

"Why the long face?" a voice purred from the grass, as Billie turned and saw that some kind of dark creature was lurking just out of sight. Only its hunched back was visible above the grass. "It's just a joke. Why so serious?"

"Janey!" Billie shouted, suddenly springing into action, gathering the sack up into her arms and then getting to her feet. "It's okay, Janey," she continued, "you're going to be fine, I promise!"

She began to carry her sister back toward the farmhouse, even as blood trickled from the sack and splattered against the ground, and as the sack's torn ends trailed in the air.

"Mom!" Billie screamed, louder than she ever thought possible, loud enough to make a flock of crows take fright at the other end of the field. "Mom, I found her! She's hurt! Mom, we have to get her to the hospital!"

"Come on, lighten up a little bit," the voice in the grass said, as the curved back shook with laughter and the ridges of its spine glinted in the morning light, and as strands of the torn sack blew across the dirt. "I didn't mean it seriously. It was just a joke!"

THE REVIEWS OF
JANET VERBLANKE

Sort by: Publication History (Oldest First)

September 12th 2019
COZY MULTI-COLORED PATCHWORK QUILT REVERSIBLE

Rating: 5 stars

I love this new quilt. My old one was getting worn out LOL which meant I got cold, but my daughter and I disagree all the time on the temperature of the house so this new one keeps my knees nice and warm in my wheelchair. Pretty pattern too.

September 12th 2019
SEE YOUR YEAR BEFORE IT HAPPENS BY AMANDA SPARROWFORD

Rating: 5 stars

I love the idea behind this book, it says you can visualize how your entire year is going to go, and then that makes it much easier to actualize (I think that's the right word) the steps you have to take in order to get the year to go that way. After the year Sylvie and I have had, with bereavements and so much else going on in our lives, I decided to get this book in the hope that it will help us turn the corner. I still need to get Sylvie interested in it, but for now I'm enjoying it a lot. Thank you.

September 15th 2019
MANADIE SIMMONS – YOU GOT ME THE WHOLE WAY ROUND (MUSIC DOWNLOAD)
Rating: 5 stars
I got this for my daughter Sylvie. I like to get her things occasionally, as a way of thanking her for all the help she gives me. She's my carer and she sacrifices so much to look after me so this is the least I can do. Not my taste of music, but she seems to love it so that's what matters LOL!

September 28th 2019
SLEEPING BAG (RED)
Rating: 5 stars
I wish I didn't have to review every purchase I make on this website. This new policy of making you review your last purchase before you make your next is very time-consuming. Anyway, this is for my

daughter Sylvie, she's spending a night out in the woods with a friend. Was a bit late arriving but came just in time, she's off tomorrow.

September 29th 2019

HOW TO SURVIVE AGORAPHOBIA IN 12 EASY STEPS BY ROGER CHRISTIAN

Rating: 5 stars

I've found this really invaluable. As an agoraphobic myself – I haven't been outside in years, or talked to anyone apart from my daughter – I was interested to learn more about how our brains work. I didn't approach it as a self help book, it's more of a chance to see how your brain makes the choices that it makes. I think this would also be excellent for anyone who wants to help a friend or family member understand their agoraphobia journey.

October 1st 2019

HOLY BIBLE – LEATHER HARDBACK EDITION

Rating: 5 stars

I don't know where my trusty old copy went. I had it for all my adult life, since I was fifteen years old, but now it's nowhere to be found in the house. Hope it turns up, it was a gift from Papa, may he rest in peace. It also had lots of little annotations that I added over the years when I wanted to save a passage for further reference later on down the line.

This one is very nice, but I do want to find my old one.

October 2ⁿᵈ 2019
SCHUBERMAIN LUXURY CAT TREATS – SALMON FLAVOR
Rating: 5 stars
Oh I thought, why not treat Mozie? Cats can have tough times too, and she seems a little skittish over the past few days. These say they're made with 100% dried fish, and you can't ask for better than that, can you? Well maybe you can if you're Mozie, after all she does like the finer things in life LOL. So far she loves them though.

October 5ᵗʰ 2019
HOLY BIBLE – LEATHER HARDBACK EDITION
Rating: 5 stars
Second new copy in a week, I honestly don't know where the last one went, it lasted all of two days before I couldn't find it again. Going to take real good care of this one LOL.

October 7ᵗʰ 2019
SCHUBERMAIN MEDIUM SIZE CAT PLAYBELL WITH ATTACHMENTS
Rating: 3 stars
Well, I think there's nothing wrong with the toy, but

I'm not entirely sure. I think Mozie is just in a really bad mood at the moment, no matter how I try to cheer her up. She's so scared, she barely comes out from under the table, and then she likes to go outside and it's almost as if she's scared of something in the house. I don't know why my little fur baby is behaving like this, but I am determined to get her back on my side LOL!

October 12th 2019
MIRACLE STAIN REMOVAL GEL, BRAND NEW 100% EFFECTIVE
Rating: 5 stars
I hope this works! Sylvie, bless her, got some of her clothes horribly dirty during a camping trip with a friend. If I'd known when she got back, I might have had better luck cleaning them, but for some reason my dear daughter stuffed the clothes in a bag under her bed and just left them there. I finally caught her trying to wash them when she thought I wasn't looking. Whatever caused it, it's a dark stain that just won't come out. The reviews on this are good, so hopefully we'll have some luck.

October 20th 2019
PLAIN WHITE DRESS SIZE M
Rating: 5 stars
My daughter needs this to attend a friend's funeral. It was in the news, how the poor girl was found

dead out in the woods. Sylvie wasn't going to go at all, but I told her she must. I can't of course, not in my wheelchair, but Sylvie has to go and pay her respects. She'll be glad she did after. She and Lana were such good friends, they went camping together not long ago. Now Lana's gone. I pray that the Lord takes her under his wing and grants her all the blessings she's due. RIP Lana Angelia Muthers 2005 to 2019, forever in our hearts.

October 30th 2019
MIRACLE STAIN REMOVAL GEL, BRAND NEW 100% EFFFECTIVE
Rating: 5 stars
Had to order more of this, Sylvie's got more stains on her clothes. I told her to maybe not go out in the woods so much, especially late at night. She's only fourteen years old, and I hear her sneaking out every night. Being a typical teenage girl, she never tells me what she's been doing.

November 5th 2019
URN FOR PET ASHES
Rating: 5 stars
Our poor darling little Mozie died this week. Something got her out in the woods, she dragged herself home but we found her on the porch. Horrible sight, half of her had been all torn away by something. We decided to have her cremated and

keep her on the sideboard.

December 10th 2019
HIDDEN EYE XTREME WIFI CAMERA
Rating: 1 star
The advert says this can be used to capture motion activated things happening at night, with night vision, but I think unit is faulty even though we returned it and had a new one sent. It keeps activating at night, but it only records for a few minutes showing the front room before it goes all grainy, like there's a static patch that moves around the screen. Completely useless. The company tried to help but I just don't think this camera works. Hoping it can catch whatever wild animal seems to be killing things in our yard.

December 20th 2019
MARK V HIDDEN CAMERA WITH WIFI RECORDING AND NIGHT VISION
Rating: 1 star
Why don't they test these things before they release them? I ordered three, on the strength of the reviews on here, and not one of them works properly! They cut out at random times in the night, usually one after the other. The one near Sylvie's bedroom door always goes first, and then it seems to bring down the others. All I want is a camera that records when it senses motion, is that so hard to make???

December 26th 2019
CHRISTMAS TABLE DECORATIONS
Rating: 5 stars
These were nice. I thought they might cheer Sylvie up, she's been so down in the dumps lately, but maybe that would have been a miracle too far. It's just me and her for Xmas again, as usual. I had a nice time, and these really brightened up the table. Sylvie said they were too sparkly, but then she's a moody teenager LOL

December 28th 2019
HOT GUARD XTRA GRIP FOR WATER BOILERS
Rating: 5 stars
Well, I had another little accident and burned my hand when I was trying to make tea. I'm not sure how it happened, something seemed to have caused the handle to get very hot. That's the third accident I've had in the house during the past week, so I guess I need to start doing something about my clumsiness.

December 28th 2019
A GUIDE TO LOOKING AFTER YOUR NEW KITTEN BY SHELLEY S. SINCLAIR
Rating: 5 stars
So we just got a new kitten, we've called her Jazz,

to replace poor Mozie. We've had kittens before, but I wanted to really get it right with this one. Mainly I bought the book for Sylvie, so she can take some more responsibility, but so far she hasn't shown much interests. Teens!

December 29th 2019
URN FOR PET ASHES
Rating: 5 stars
This is very sad. Our new kitten lasted one day before something out there got her. She wasn't even supposed to be let outside yet, but Sylvia accidentally left the door open. Next thing you know, little Jazz is all torn up and spread across the yard in the morning. I honestly don't know what could have caused that, but I don't want to get another pet until we know.

December 30th 2019
MIRACLE STAIN REMOVAL GEL, BRAND NEW 100% EFFECTIVE
Rating: 5 stars
Second tub of this I've bought recently, used the first tub up after Sylvie started getting all messy during her nocturnal trips into the wood. Honestly, that girl is becoming quite a rascal.

December 30th 2019
HOLY BIBLE – LEATHER HARDBACK

EDITION

Rating: 5 stars

Well, that's the third copy of the good book that I've had to buy this year. My original went missing, then the second went missing, and then the next copy just ended up all torn up, I don't have any idea how. It's almost like it exploded off the shelf, there were pages everywhere. Is there something wrong with the spine? I hope this copy lasts me longer.

January 5th 2020

XTRA SECURE DOOR BOLT

Rating: 5 stars

I bought this for my bedroom door, to secure it from the inside. Hard to install but it seems sturdy enough.

January 10th 2020

TRUE HORROR CRIME: THE POWER OF SATAN IN YOUR LIFE (120mins, rated R)

Rating: 1 star

I did not order or download this movie! I do not know why it is on my account! I have no interest in this kind of filth! Please, will you take it off my account and give me my money back?

January 13th 2020

SOUND RECORDER WITH WIFI CONNECTIVITY

Rating: 3 stars

Not sure if this works or not, or if I'm just not using it right. Quite complicated to set up. Captures sounds well enough in the middle of the night, but then the audio quality isn't great. What sounds like voices comes out as hisses and static, so it's hard to know what I'm really capturing. It does seem to work in general, though, I'm just not sure it's right for my needs.

January 25th 2020

SATANISM IN THE TWENTY-FIRST CENTURY (136 mins, rated R)

Rating: 1 star

I DID NOT ORDER THIS! WHY ARE YOU CHARGING ME FOR THIS, I DO NOT DOWNLOAD MOVIES, I DO NOT EVEN KNOW HOW TO DO THAT OR HOW TO WATCH THEM! SCAM!

January 30th 2020

DURABLE OUTDOOR CAMERA – ALL WEATHER

Rating: 3 stars

I had to set this up myself. It's for monitoring the door that leads onto the porch, so I can see what keeps bringing the dead animals out of the woods. So far it seems very buggy, it always seems to cut out just as something appears. I've tried fine-tuning it but I haven't had much luck so far. Not sure if the problem is the camera or something else.

February 1st 2020

SIMPLE WOODEN CRUCIFIX

Rating: 5 stars

I wanted something simple, not flash, and that's what I got.

February 10th 2020

DEMONS AMONG US: 10 SUREFIRE SIGNS OF POSSESSION BY MICHAEL V. MAKKEVICH

Rating: 1 star

I would give this zero stars if I could, it's all made up, I thought it was factual but it's like someone just watched some stupid TV shows and wrote down what happens. I feel ripped off.

February 11th 2020

A BRIEF HISTORY OF EXORCISM IN THE UNITED STATES BY S.R. BURGOYNE

Rating: 5 stars

Very hard to read, small text and a very academic style, but interesting. Talks about how exorcisms are up in numbers over the past few years, and offers ideas about why that might be happening. I wish it had more information about how to head things off before they get bad, but it's not really supposed to be that sort of book so I can't complain too much. Anyway, I just was interested, that's all.

February 15th 2020
LATIN TO ENGLISH DICTIONARY
Rating: 2 stars
This is probably okay if you need to translate from a book, but there's not much information about pronunciation so it's useless if you want to translate something you overheard.

February 20th 2020
SOUND RECORDER WITH WIFI CONNECTIVITY
Rating: 1 star
Second one of these I've bought, after the first went missing. Big mistake! I set it up to record, came to check it this morning and it had completely melted to nothing. Lucky it didn't start a fire!

February 20th 2020
THE KILLING PLACE: A CONVERSATION WITH REAL SATANISTS (91 mins, rated R)
Rating: 1
I HAVE CHANGED MY PASSWORD THREE TIMES NOW I DID NOT ORDER THIS I DO NOT WANT IT ON MY ACCOUNT PLEASE TAKE IT OFF IMMEDIATELY! I DON'T UNDERSTAND WHY YOUR WEBSITE

PRETENDS I'M WATCHING THESE TYPES OF MOVIES, I COME TO MY COMPUTER SOME MORNINGS AND THEY'RE JUST THERE! STOP! I WILL CHANGE MY PASSWORD AGAIN!

February 21st 2020
SIMPLE WOODEN CRUCIFIX
Rating: 5 stars
Had to replace one that went missing.

February 23rd 2020
SIMPLE WOODEN CRUCIFIX
Rating: 5 stars
I've already reviewed this, why do I have to review it again? I just wish they wouldn't keep going missing!

February 28th 2020
SIMPLE WOODEN CRUCIFIX
Rating: 5 stars
I'm starting to think that these evaporate. They just disappear from my bedroom and I don't know why!

March 1st 2020
SIMPLE WOODEN CRUCIFIX
Rating: 1 star
Something must be wrong with them because they always vanish within twenty-four hours of coming

into my home. Is it some kind of trick to make us buy more? I'm no sucker!

March 3rd 2020

XTRA SECURE DOOR BOLT WITH ADDED GUARD

Rating: 5 stars

The last one I bought was good, or I thought so, but now I'm starting to think it can be tampered with and opened from the other side. I'm not sure how, but that seems to have been happening, so I'm hoping this one will be better.

March 10th 2020

Rating: 5 stars

HOLY BIBLE – LEATHER HARDBACK EDITION

My last one went missing again.

March 12th 2020

Rating: 5 stars

HOLY BIBLE – LEATHER HARDBACK EDITION

What is with these things and how they keep vanishing on me?

March 17th 2020

HOLY BIBLE – LEATHER HARDBACK EDITION

Rating: 1 star

Flammable! Just caught fire one night, all by itself, on the shelf in my room!

March 20th 2020

HOLY BIBLE – LEATHER HARDBACK EDITION

Rating: 1 star

They should not sell these. They keep combusting spontaneously, when they're not even being touched! Something is wrong with them, I don't know where they're made but they must be using some kind of weird chemical in the paper. Stop selling them immediately!

March 21st 2020

HOLY BIBLE – LEATHER HARDBACK EDITION

Rating: 1 star

EXTREMELY FLAMMABLE!

March 21st 2020

NVR-BURN HAND CREAM FOR LIGHT BURNS

Rating: 5 stars

Very soothing, especially at night. When the mailman came with these to the mailbox at the end of our yard, I very nearly went out there and took the package straight from him. And I say that as someone who's agoraphobic and who does everything in her power to avoid meeting strangers. But this is the good stuff, I must say, even if I have to use a lot on my hands.

March 27th 2020

DELUXE BIBLE – HARDBACK

Rating: 1 star

This one melted! Does no-one have any standards these days? What is wrong with people?

March 28th 2020

EXORCISMS AT HOME: A GUIDE TO RIDDING YOUR HOME OF SPIRITS BY SUSAN BOWYLER

Rating: 5 stars

I've given this five stars, but I'm not so sure whether it works yet or not. Seems to have a lot of practical advice, but I guess it takes time to see whether that's going to actually help.

April 10th 2020

XTRA SECURE DOOR BOLT WITH ADDED GUARD

Rating: 5 stars

Bought six more, to use at various points around the door. I like that they can only be opened using a special key, and although that takes time when you have so many on one door, it does give you a feeling of security.

April 22nd 2020
15-INCH CHEF'S KNIFE
Rating: 5 stars
Seems sturdy enough.

April 22nd 2020
15 FT ROPE
Rating: 5 stars
I am getting sick of having to review everything. What can I say about a rope? It's long and it seems strong, but I won't know if it's strong enough until I have to use it, will I? Which I hope I won't!

April 22nd 2020
HOCKEY MASK – WHITE – SIZE M
Rating: 5 stars
The straps seem fairly strong so hopefully they would hold even if for example someone was trying to bash them open.

April 30th 2020
HOLY WATER – 50CL
Rating: 5 stars
It's ridiculous that I had to buy this online. Comes with a certificate that promises it is what it says it is, and I can only trust that this is true. Also I hate that you can only buy it in 50 cl vials, so I have had to

buy 20 of these vials in order to have remotely enough.

May 1ˢᵗ 2020
HOW TO CONDUCT AN EXORCISM BY VARIOUS

Rating: 5 stars

This isn't so much one way to conduct an exorcism, as different accounts by different practitioners telling you how they do it. From those accounts, it's possible to build up a kind of idea of the main aspects, even if I'd rather have a more authoritative guide that just sets it out easily like 'do this', then 'do that' etc. Why is that so hard?

May 1ˢᵗ 2020
TIGER 50 PACK OF SLEEPING TABLETS

Rating: 5 stars

Really surprised I could buy these on here, but I guess there must be some local law that allows it. Super glad. Only was allowed to buy one pack, which I understand.

May 10ᵗʰ 2020
EARPLUGS – EXTRA POWERFUL (10 PACK)

Rating: 5 stars

These work quite well, they block out most of the sounds that I need to block out, although some of the more high-pitched ones still get through. I think they do as well as you can really expect.

May 17th 2020
HOLY BIBLE
Rating: 1 star
Even more flammable than the other one!

May 20th 2020
PACK OF 100 RUBBER BANDS
Rating: 5 stars
I don't know why I bought these, really. I don't need them. I watched out the window until the mailman appeared. Our box is a couple hundred feet from the porch, so I can just about see him. I thought about going out there and saying something to him, but I couldn't quite summon the courage. I eventually fetched the rubber bands after he was gone. I feel a little foolish for that now, and now I have one hundred rubber bands that I don't need.

May 25th 2020
HOLY WATER – 50CL
Rating: 3 stars
I don't even know if this is real holy water! If it is, it doesn't seem to work like it should! I don't believe that anyone would try to scam other people by selling fake holy water, but this just acts like normal water! Now I don't know if I'm doing something wrong or if it's the water that's wrong!

May 30th 2020
CRUCIFIX
Rating: 5 stars
I have purchased fifty of these, which was quite expensive but also not too bad considering how many I needed. They are easy to hang up even when you are in a wheelchair.

May 31st 2020
THE GANNON GUIDE TO HEALTH IN THE HOME BY THE GANNON INSTITUTE
Rating: 3 stars
What I don't understand is why this doesn't have specific information about things like nutrition. It has all the usual information that you'd expect, but it doesn't explain for example how you can make sure that someone gets everything they need when they refuse to eat. Isn't that the sort of thing you'd want in a book like this? I guess you can try to work it out, but that's not what I want, I want actual factual information.

June 14th 2020
MIRACLE STAIN REMOVAL GEL, BRAND NEW 100% EFFECTIVE
Rating: 5 stars
For white bed sheets this time.

June 15th 2020
ODOR NEUTRALIZER (PINK)
Rating: 5 stars
This does a good job. You place it by the door, it stops any smells coming from the other side of the door.

June 20th 2020
LAVENDER SCENTED CANDLES (PACK OF 30)
Rating: 5 stars
I have always loved the smell of lavender and now the whole house smells of it. I keep one of these lit at all times in the house and it does the trick, at least it does for now.

June 29th 2020
SALT
Rating: 5 stars
Because I could only order small bags, I had to order several of them, but now I have what I consider to be enough. For now, at least. Enough to draw a line around an entire bed.

June 30th 2020
XTRA STRONG LAVENDER SCENTED CANDLES – PACK OF 100
Rating: 5 stars
The previous ones I bought turned out to not be

strong enough, not even when you lit a whole lot of them at once, so I am trying these ones because the other reviews are so good. I don't know if 100 is enough but we will have to wait and see, I hope the smell is really strong.

July 3rd 2020
ULTRAMETRONIX DEHUMIDIFIER (PORTABLE)
Rating: 5 stars
Small but effective, although I'm not sure that it's what I really need. I read that these can sometimes help with bad odors.

July 10th 2020
THE LORD IS ALWAYS WITH YOU BY ADRIAN KELOCHES
Rating: 5 stars
This book is invaluable. At my lowest point, it has shown me that the Lord is always here with me and that He will get me through everything. Also, that He knows the truth in my heart, and that He does not judge us when we do things in His name. He knows when we are on the side of right, and he does not judge those whose souls have fallen to darkness. I can only pray that this book by Mr. Adrian Keloches is right. I have read it all the way through five times now in just two days and it has given me great relief to know in my heart that He understands

the actions of everybody. No matter what anyone might think, He is with us every step of the way. It is He, and only He, who will judge us when that day comes. Which means sometimes you've just got to pick yourself up, stop feeling sorry for yourself, and get on with the task at hand. Amen.

July 20th 2020
SHOVEL
Rating: 1 star
This is no good for someone like me who is in a wheelchair, it is supposed to be specifically for people with back and mobility problems but it is taking me so long to dig what should be a simple hole to dig! Even then, it's probably the best that I can get, I just wish that the manufacturers would think of people like me!

July 21st 2020
NATURAL RELAXATION TABLETS WITH GINSENG, GINGER AND ESSENTIAL MINERALS – PACK OF 30
Rating: 5 stars
These are the only thing that can really get me to sleep at the moment, without having nightmares.

July 22nd 2020
SIMPLE CLOTH SACK (LARGE)
Rating: 5 stars

I don't know what I was expecting, but I love how simple this is, almost elegant. It ties at one end, with a simple string that is both delicate and strong, which I think is a good combination.

July 25th 2020
SILVER NECKLACE – HEART SHAPE – SIMPLE CHAIN
Rating: 5 stars
Sylvie would have loved this. I thought, on her birthday, I should get something for her, even if she can no longer appreciate it. She always preferred simple, discreet jewelry, and I truly believe that this would have been one of her favorites. I wish that somehow, wherever she is, she might be able to see that I still love the sweet girl she was before.

July 30th 2020
SILVER PICTURE FRAME
Rating: 5 stars
This is lovely and tasteful, a simple frame that doesn't mess around with lots of stupid embellishments. There's even a little window beneath the main photo area, so you can add an inscription if you so wish. Of course you need a printer if you want to do this, although I chose to make it handwritten which I think is so much more fitting.

August 10th 2020

HOPE FOR THE FUTURE: A GUIDE TO OPTIMISM AFTER A TRAGEDY BY DOCTOR BERNARD F. FALL

Rating: 5 stars

This is such a wonderful book that I would recommend to anyone who has been through a difficult time. Doctor Fall has many years of experience dealing with this sort of thing and he shows how you can accept what has happened while still moving on with your life. This is especially useful if you are dealing with a lot of guilt, which let's face it many of us are, some even more than others. If you are struggling, please give Doctor Fall's invaluable book a read, because I truly believe it will change your life just as it changed mine. Bless him.

August 19th 2020

PINK PLUSH CUSHION

Rating: 5 stars

This is lovely, and the color really goes well with my drapes. I've been trying to cheer myself up lately, and sometimes it's the simple things in life that do that better than anything big or expensive.

August 25th 2020

GREECE: A GUIDE FOR TRAVELERS BY THE CRAZY PLANET MONGO TEAM

Rating: 3 stars

I found this guide useful, but only to a certain degree. As a disabled woman of a certain age, I face various challenges if I am ever to go on vacation alone. I know that one day I can beat my agoraphobia and then I want to see the world. This book does not really offer much advice for someone such as myself, although it is of course filled with inspiration about where in particular to visit. To be honest, I think all these thoughts of a vacation are really just a way to daydream away the hours.

September 1st 2020

SUPER MEGA VOX WEEDKILLER TURBO 5000 (LARGE PACK)

Rating: 3 stars

While I have no doubt that this weedkiller is very potent, it does seem to struggle with the strange little white round flowers that have begun to poke up in a certain spot in my garden. Everything else dies immediately, but if anything the little white flowers almost seem to feed on the weedkiller and get stronger. I must find something better.

September 5th 2020

COMMUNICATING WITH THE DEAD BY LOUISE ALLAMATTERHORN

Rating: 2 stars

This book claims to be about how to make contact

with those you have lost, particularly if you are trying to ascertain whether they are angry with you. In practice, while the book might work for some people, I feel that its advice can't easily be adapted to unusual situations.

September 8th 2020

A GUIDE TO UNUSUAL PLANTS AND BLOOMS BY DOCTOR HENRY L. LITTENBAUM

Rating: 3 stars

While this is a lovely book, with wonderful illustrations, it has failed to identify the white flowers that are blossoming all around my house. They bring with them a peculiar, rather nasty smell, and they are impossible to kill. I had hoped that this book might help me to identify them, but alas I am back at square one.

September 9th 2020

GARLIC AND HERB BUNDLES (PACK OF SIX)

Rating: 5 stars

These are supposed to ward off evil spirits. There are six in the pack, so I used two for the doors and I put the other four on various windows. They come highly recommended, and the other reviews say that they can really work wonders. I only hope that they do indeed offer some level of protection.

September 12th 2020
FLASHLIGHT – BLACK
Rating: 5 stars
Seems good.

September 12th 2020
DSF8498 DIGITAL CAMERA WITH ENHANCED NIGHT VISION CAPABILITIES
Rating: 5 stars
So far, out of the box, it seems good. The image is slightly grainy, especially on video compared to still photos. The battery lasts me almost all night, only have to plug it in when the sun comes up, so that's good enough. Takes all day to charge again but I only need it at night.

September 12th 2020
HOW TO KILL ZOMBIES! BY BEN SULLIVAN
Rating: 5 stars
I will review this book tomorrow once I have seen whether or not it works.

THE BOILER

Rain crashed down, hammering the road and the parked cars and the houses on either side of Sandown Street, battering the loose tin roof of a shed in somebody's garden, hitting windows and running down drainpipes before splashing out into gutters.

Evening had turned the sky a dark shade of blue, almost black, and finally a little after 5pm the heavens had opened. Anyone who wasn't already home had found a place to shelter, waiting for the abominable storm to pass. Only a fool, or a madman, or a desperate man would risk getting caught outside in such an onslaught. Most of the shops in town were shut, but anyone who happened to have been trapped in a pub figured they were obliged to have another drink and wait for the onslaught to be over.

Sitting in his van, Sam watched as the clock on the digital dash ticked over to 17:05. He was five minutes late for his final appointment of the day, but – although he could see the house on the other side of the road – he figured he should wait a little while longer, just in case the weather eased. Besides, this visit to Mr. Luckit's house wasn't officially an appointment at all, it was more of a quick job off the books on the way home. He checked his phone again and saw the forecast, which showed the same terrible conditions continuing well into the small hours, and then he looked at the house again. The lights were on downstairs, and he knew full well that he was about to get into trouble for being late.

Mr. Luckit *always* found something to complain about.

All around, rain battered the tarmac and the car, falling with an interminable rhythm that seemed to have a voice of its own. As Sam continued to stare at the house, he began to think that he could hear the rain speaking to him, telling him to turn around and go home. No job, the rain hissed, was worth so much aggravation. Anyone else would have told Mr. Luckit to shove his stupid boiler somewhere rather unfortunate. And, the rain seemed to say, it was doing its bit by trying to force him back, by trying to make him turn around and go home. The worst part was that Sam knew the rain was right.

He glanced at the clock again.

5.09pm.

Suddenly his phone buzzed, and he saw that Mr. Luckit was trying to get through. Glancing at the house again, he saw a figure stepping back from the window, letting the net curtain fall. Sam hesitated for a moment, and then he bowed to the inevitable and answered the call.

"Sam," Mr. Luckit snapped with his usual abruptness, "where are you? You were supposed to be here ten minutes ago. Are you coming or not?"

"I'm right outside," he replied, and a moment later he saw the front door open and a head pop out. Evidently Mr. Luckit didn't want to admit that he'd been at the window. "I just parked up."

"Well, then get your ass in here now!" Mr. Luckit said angrily. "I'm sick and tired of your incompetence, Sam! If you don't manage to finally get this boiler fixed tonight, I'll be taking my custom elsewhere *and* I'll make sure that everyone in this town knows that you're an absolutely pathetic plumber! Do I make myself clear?"

"I'll be right in," Sam replied, bristling slightly even though he was well accustomed to Mr. Luckit's abrasive nature. "I'm just getting my tools together."

He heard Mr. Luckit huffing and puffing on the other end of the line, but a moment later the call was cut. Sighing, Sam realized that he still had one last chance to drive away and let somebody else fix Mr. Luckit's recalcitrant boiler, but then he reminded himself that he couldn't afford to have his name tarnished, not in such a small town. And Mr. Luckit, he knew, was most certainly not the kind of person to issue an empty threat. Sighing again, he reached over and grabbed his toolbox, and then he hesitated before opening the door and stepping out into the monsoon.

The rain, so much louder now, warned him one final time to turn back.

***

Standing in the deluge, next to a drainpipe that was pouring rainwater onto the pavement, Sam waited for the front door to open. He'd rung the bell thirty seconds, maybe a minute earlier, but so far nobody had answered. He knew that ringing again would infuriate Mr. Luckit, but he was getting absolutely soaked and he was starting to fear that he was the victim of some stubborn practical joke. Either that, or Mr. Luckit was trying to make some point about tardiness.

Finally the door opened, and light from the hallway bathed Sam's rain-lashed face.

"Ah," Mr. Luckit said with a faint smile, "you made it. Wonderful. Sorry to keep you waiting. It's not a nice feeling, is it?"

Sam stared at him for a moment, before Mr. Luckit stepped aside and gestured for him to go inside.

"Don't forget to take your shoes off," Mr. Luckit added. "The last thing I want is all that mud and dirt on my carpet."

As soon as he was in the hallway, Sam set his toolbox down and started peeling his raincoat off, and then he took off his shoes. Glancing over at the door, he saw Mrs. Luckit and her son Dean staring at him with blank, perhaps slightly apprehensive expressions. Mrs. Luckit and Dean always seemed to be loitering, almost on show, whenever Sam visited the house. They never seemed to be very relaxed.

"Good evening," he said, trying to remain polite.

Mrs. Luckit merely offered a faint, almost imperceptible smile. She was sporting a black eye, which was only partially covered by make-up. Dean, meanwhile, remained impassive, as if some part of him had been shut off from the rest of the world.

"You'd better come through," Mr. Luckit said, leading him toward the door past the stairs. "As I told you over the phone, this bloody boiler is still playing up. Last night, we were woken by the most terrible banging sound, and the hot water's completely unreliable. When you fixed this thing on

Monday, Sam, you assured me that you'd finally located the problem that's been plaguing us for the past three months. It would appear that yet again you were wrong and you've left us with a defective unit. I mean, is it really so hard to find a fault and repair it?"

"I'm really sorry, Mr. Luckit," he replied, following him through to the utility room and then stopping as he saw the boiler on the far wall. "I was sure I'd fixed it last time."

The boiler, a fairly old unit that was nevertheless well within its expected lifespan, seemed almost to stare back at him. The pressure indicator formed one eye, while the manufacturer's logo formed the other, and below those there was a large control panel that looked like a kind of mouth.

"This is the sixth time you've been out to fix this thing in three months," Mr. Luckit said, clearly unimpressed as they both stared at the boiler. "I don't know what's going on, Sam, but I'm starting to run out of patience. I don't want to have to find another plumber, because your father and I are old friends and it'd be very awkward if I had to stop using you, but you clearly haven't managed to figure out what's wrong with this thing. Please, you have to promise me that you'll get it fixed this time. Whatever's wrong with it, just track the problem down and sort it out. For the love of God, I'm sick of all this messing around."

"I'll sort it out," Sam replied, feeling a little embarrassed. After all, Mr. Luckit had a point, even if it was one that he was expressing in a very strident manner. Sam definitely felt as if the boiler had been defeating him. "Whatever's going on, I won't rest until I've located the fault this time. You have my word."

"I had your word last time," Mr. Luckit said as he checked his watch. "Listen, I'm taking my wife and son out for dinner and a film, we'll be gone about four hours. Please try to have this thing under control by the time we get back. You can show yourself out. Obviously I won't be paying your usual fee for this call-out, seeing as how I paid you for the first visit and you still haven't actually solved the problem."

"Sure," Sam replied, forcing a smile. "That's totally fair."

"I can't believe the damn thing can be *this* complicated," Mr. Luckit continued as he headed to the door and then stopped to look back at Sam. "It's only a boiler. Oh, and if you need the bathroom, use the one downstairs, okay? And if you want a glass of water, there are glasses in the cupboard by the sink."

"Okay," Sam said.

"This boiler," Mr. Luckit muttered, "is... I don't know, sometimes I think it doesn't *want* to get fixed."

With that, he left the room, leaving Sam to turn back to look at the boiler and try to figure out what was wrong this time. In each of his previous visits, there'd seemed to be some new fault, something that he couldn't explain. If he didn't know better, he'd have started to think that the damn thing was being sabotaged, although deep down he knew that wasn't possible. There had to be something he was missing, some root problem that was manifesting in all the dramatically different problems that were causing so many call-outs. Something that was making the wretched thing seem almost alive, like some kind of infernal trickster.

As he heard the Luckits leaving the house, and the front door slamming shut, Sam set his toolbox down and took a deep breath. This time, he was determined to get to the root of the problem once and for all.

***

"Nothing there," he muttered an hour later, as he finished examining the pump. Having convinced himself that he'd find a fresh crack, he was a little disappointed to discover that his latest theory had fallen flat. After all, a cracked pump would have explained the problem, and would also have been fairly easy to fix.

Then again, he'd already replaced the pump once, and that hadn't resolved the problem. Already, Sam was resorting to wild guesses.

Sighing, he stepped back and took another look at the stripped-down boiler. He'd already run through all his usual checks, none of which had shown any indication of the problem, and now he was starting to feel totally stumped. On all his previous call-outs, he'd found fairly simple issues with the boiler, albeit issues that were supposed to be entirely unconnected and issues that he was sure hadn't been there before. This time something more tricky was clearly occurring, and he was starting to feel a little pressure. After all, he knew that he had to come up with a solution by the time Mr. Luckit returned home, which meant that he was going to have to scour every millimeter of the boiler in search of whatever had gone wrong. And if that didn't work...

"It *will* work," he said out loud, determined to maintain a positive attitude. "I've never been defeated by a boiler yet, and I'm not going to start now."

Those words almost, sort of, kind of made him feel a little more confident. He set to work again, meticulously examining the boiler's pipe and wire and connection.

Every few minutes, a faint rumbling sound rang out from somewhere within the system, but

Sam had already checked the house's radiators and he was sure that the problem had to be situated in the boiler itself. He forced himself to work slowly, taking care to not overlook even the tiniest component even though he was sure he'd been thorough already. After a while, he noticed that the rumbling sound was becoming a little more urgent, although it was still nothing too concerning. And then, finally, just as he was starting to think that he was on a hiding to nothing, he discovered the tiniest crack on one of the connections located on the rear of the timer. In that instant, he began to have hope that he might actually have found the solution, although he was also certain that there had been no crack there on his previous visit.

"That could be it," he whispered, leaning closer, and after a moment he felt a rush of relief as he realized that he'd located the problem. "Thank you, God!"

Stepping back, he thought for a moment of all the pieces of spare kit in his van, and he quickly realized that by some miracle he had a spare timer that would fit perfectly. Of course, he'd been convinced he'd solved the problem on every previous visit, too, but this time he was absolutely sure that he knew what was wrong. The track on the timer explained almost everything. Even as the thudding and hissing continued inside the boiler, he was running through the options in his mind, and he soon realized that he should be able to get the new timer installed well before Mr. Luckit and his family returned from the cinema. The saga would finally be over. Turning, he began to make his way to the door.

"Let me."

He stopped suddenly, convinced that he had to be mistaken, that the boiler's strange sounds had not just somehow twisted and contorted themselves to form those two hissed words. Slowly he turned and looked over his shoulder, and he saw the boiler with all its innards and gubbins exposed, and with the main panel – the part bearing the face-like pattern – resting on the floor. For a moment he felt as if something was watching him, but he quickly forced himself to get a grip, and the sensation passed.

He waited a moment, and then he hurried out of the room, determined to fetch the spare timer from his van and then get to work, and to be long gone by the time Mr. Luckit returned.

***

"Okay, my friend," he said once he'd brought the timer inside and set his toolbox on the shelf next to the boiler, "time to get you fixed."

Reaching around the underside of the unit with a screwdriver, he fumbled for a moment to find the first screw. He glanced up at the boiler and thought back to the strange voice that he'd seemed to have heard, and he quickly reminded himself that the whole thing was impossible. The boiler was just a boiler, so he focused on trying to remove the screw. As he did that, he heard the boiler clanking and rumbling again, before once more the same two words seemed to fill the air.

"Let me."

This time Sam waited a little longer, and he couldn't deny the fact that he was somewhat freaked out by what had just happened. The voice, which he knew couldn't actually be real, had nevertheless seemed very clear, especially this second time. Sure, he'd noticed earlier how the rain had seemed to be speaking, but he'd been fully aware at that time that he was simply enjoying a little poetic license. Daydreaming, perhaps. This time, however, the boiler's hisses and gurgles had definitely seemed to be conspiring to speak. Still, he'd only heard it twice, and he told himself this had to be a coincidence. So long as it didn't happen for a third time, everything would be fine.

He hesitated, and then he moved the screwdriver's tip closer to the screw and began to turn. He was tense with anticipation, worried that he'd hear the voice again and also praying that he wouldn't.

"Let me do it."

Startled, Sam pulled back, dropping the screwdriver in the process. His heart was pounding, and he could still hear rain falling outside, and as he stared at the boiler he realized that somehow it *had* spoken to him.

"You keep stopping me," the hissing voice continued, as several pipes clanged and shifted. "Please, you have to let me do this."

Sam opened his mouth to reply, but no words left his lips. He was starting to think that he must have lost his mind, and after a moment he reached into his pocket to grab his phone, figuring that he needed to call his sister and ask her for help. After all, she worked as a therapist, so he told himself that she'd know exactly what to do. He couldn't be the first person who'd ever heard a voice coming from an inanimate object, and he figured there were probably some pills that would make everything better again. There was always a pill.

He took a deep breath.

"I won't hurt the others," the voice said suddenly. "Only him."

Again Sam opened his mouth to reply, and again he stopped himself at the last second. Replying, he told himself, would only make the absurd hallucination seem more real, would add fuel to the fire. Looking down at his phone, he brought up his sister's number, but then he froze as he realized how utterly ridiculous the story would sound. How would he even persuade her that he was serious? How could he explain the story without coming across as an utter lunatic?

"I see what he does to them," the voice continued, its tone changing as the hissing sound continued. The timer, dangling by wires, shook slightly. "He always brings them in here, because he doesn't want to do it in the rest of the house. He calls this the other room. He says that what happens in here, stays in here. He says it's private, just between them, but that's not true. *I* see it all."

Staring at the boiler, Sam began to wonder whether he was being subjected to some kind of bizarre prank. Was this Mr. Luckit's way of teaching him some strange lesson about tardiness? He hesitated for a moment longer, before rushing forward and desperately searching for some kind of hidden speaker somewhere in the boiler's casing. He reached inside frantically, convinced that a speaker had to be just out of sight.

"You don't believe me," the hissing voice said suddenly.

Letting out a cry of shock, Sam pulled away, almost tripping and falling backward in the process.

"Be honest," the voice continued, "you don't really think this is happening, do you?"

Sam swallowed hard.

"*Well*?" the voice asked. "Say something."

Sam looked around the room for a moment,

and then back at the boiler. There was absolutely no way that he wanted to talk to the damn thing, and somewhere at the back of his mind he was still clinging to the hope – however desperate – that he was simply experiencing a string of rather odd coincidences.

"Let me keep this simple," the voice continued. "One day, when that monster is all alone in the house, I'm going to put a stop to his actions. In order to do that, I need to manifest a fault, something I can use against him. Every time I come close, he calls you in to fix me, and you end up setting my work back. I can't stop you fixing my timer today, but I'm begging you to stay away next time he calls you. Just a day or two longer should be enough. This man does awful things to his wife and child, right here in this room in front of me. I know how to stop him. I have a plan. Please, let me do it."

The pipes continued to hiss for a few more seconds, before falling silent.

Sam waited, terrified that the voice would come back at any moment, but finally he realized that the strange encounter seemed to be over. He still hesitated, half wondering whether some unusual gas had caused him to imagine things, but then he looked at the damaged timer and he realized that he could get the job done and leave the house inside half an hour if he just worked fast. Worried about somehow causing the voice to start again, he briefly considered leaving immediately, and then he forced himself to get to work.

His hands were trembling slightly as he started removing the old timer, but thankfully the pipes remained quiet now and the voice did not return. There was one final hiss, a few minutes later, that almost sounded like the word "Please," but Sam put that thought well and truly out of his mind.

***

"Well, it seems fine now," Mr. Luckit muttered later, as he stood with Sam in the utility room and stared at the boiler, "but we thought that a few times before, didn't we?"

He turned to Sam.

"Are you sure it was the timer?"

Sam watched the boiler for a moment with a slightly suspicious expression, worried that it might start talking again, and then he turned to Mr. Luckit.

"I'm sure," he stammered. "I mean, yes. I mean..."

His voice trailed off. He hadn't mentioned the voice at all, and already he was starting to think that the whole thing must have been some kind of illusion, that he'd endured a kind of 'episode' or breakdown.

"Well, you might as well get going," Mr. Luckit said finally. "I'm serious, Sam, if this thing causes more problems in a day or two, I'm going to be *very* unimpressed. You can understand that, can't you? My time is very valuable, and I've already wasted far too much of it trying to get *you* to do your job properly."

"Of course," Sam said, trying but failing to offer a smile. "I'm sure it was the timer. Really sure. I've replaced it now and everything should be as good as new. Better, even."

He still eyed the boiler with suspicion.

"I hope you're right," Mr. Luckit said, and then he turned and began to lead Sam out into the hallway. "You know, I like you. You remind me of your father, and he's always been a good man. I might have some more work for you down the line, once I've finalized the purchase of the hotel. For me to trust you with that work, however, I need to know that I can rely on you, and this saga with the boiler has given me a few doubts. You can understand where I'm coming from, Sam, can't you?"

Reaching the front door, Sam turned to him. Before he could say anything, however, he spotted Mrs. Luckit sitting on the sofa in the front room, staring into space. He could still see that she was using makeup in an attempt to cover a black eye, and after a moment he began to think back to the voice that he'd heard earlier in the evening.

"You must forgive my wife," Mr. Luckit

said, stepping over and pulling the living room door shut. "She's very tired. We went to see a rather loud film, for the benefit of Dean. He enjoyed it, but Deborah and I have emerged a little shaken by all the flash-bangs and the wallops. We're just going to have a nice glass of wine and relax for a little while, and then it'll be time for an early night."

He paused, before reaching past Sam and opening the front door. Outside, rain was still lashing down.

"Goodnight, Sam," he added.

"Goodnight," Sam replied, feeling a little bewildered as he stepped outside.

Stopping on the pavement, bathed in the light from the house, he turned back to look at Mr. Luckit. Even as rain poured down and drenched him once again, Sam considered that perhaps he *should* mention the voice after all. Sure, he knew he'd end up sounding like a lunatic, but he figured he had a duty to mention the weirdness that he'd experienced. He just needed to work out exactly how to start the conversation without immediately coming across as a complete idiot.

"Uh, Mr. Luckit," he said cautiously, "I think -"

"Goodnight, Sam."

With that, Mr. Luckit swung the door shut, leaving Sam standing alone in the darkness and the rain. All around, the rain was battering the road and the parked cars and the pavement with the same rapid rhythm as before. Water was running fast down drainpipes, and a moment later a car drove past the end of the road, splashing through puddles that had collected in potholes. The noise of the rainstorm was relentless, but there was no voice emerging from the hissing and the tapping and the dripping. There was just a wall of sound, and as Sam turned and carried his toolbox back to his van he felt relieved that at least the rain wasn't talking to him.

Perhaps, he figured, his moment of madness was over.

***

Three weeks later, standing in Mrs. Warbuthnott's kitchen, Sam admired his latest work.

"That looks wonderful," Mrs. Warbuthnott said, as they both stared at the newly installed boiler. "I can't believe it only took you five hours!"

"It was more or less a straight swap," he told her with a smile. "There was very little work to do to the pipes. I think you'll be really pleased with this model, it's my go-to brand, I've never known anyone have a problem with them. Do you need me to show you again how to use the timer on the wall in your living room, or do you think you've got that figured out?"

"Oh, I'll muddle through," she replied. "Can I offer you another cup of tea before you go?"

"I'm fine, thank you," he told her. "I have another job to get to. I'll just tidy all this mess up, and then I'll be out of your hair."

As Mrs. Warbuthnott shuffled out of the kitchen, Sam set to work gathering all his tools. He always felt a sense of real satisfaction whenever he completed a big job, and the installation of Mrs. Warbuthnott's new boiler had gone without a hitch. Crouching down, he began to close up his toolbox, and then he felt his phone buzzing in his pocket. Pulling it out, he saw to his surprise that his father was trying to get in touch.

"Hey Dad," he said as he answered, "I'm just finishing up a job, can I call you later?"

"Jacob Luckit is dead."

Sam opened his mouth to reply, but then he felt a shiver pass through his chest as those four words hit home.

"Sorry?" he stammered.

"I just heard," his father continued. "Apparently his wife found him this morning, they think he died over the weekend while she and their son were visiting her mother. Nothing's confirmed, but it looks like there might have been a carbon monoxide leak from his boiler." He paused. "Sam, I know Jacob Luckit sometimes liked to get people to do jobs for him off the books, so to speak. Under the counter, cheaper and without the paperwork. He didn't get you to work on his boiler at any point recently, did he?"

"Me?"

Feeling his heart starting to race, Sam thought back to that strange moment in the Luckits' utility room, when he'd thought the boiler was talking to him.

"You didn't do any work on that boiler, Sam, did you?" his father asked. "Come on, son, this is important."

"No," Sam lied, figuring that he needed time to think. "I didn't... No, I didn't touch it."

"Thank the Lord," his father said with a relieved sigh. "I know you probably hadn't, but I wanted to make sure. That man could be such a... Well, I won't speak ill of him, not now he's gone. It's a real shock, I've known him most of my life. He had his faults, but fifty-two is way too early for anyone to go. I can't imagine what poor Debbie and Dean are going through."

"Dad, I've got to go," Sam replied, struggling to keep from panicking. "I'll call you later."

He cut the call before his father could reply, and then he remained completely motionless as he thought back to that strange visit to Mr. Luckit's house. Everything had been done under the counter, as his father had suggested, and Sam knew that he'd left no paper trail that could officially connect him to that boiler. At the same time, he also knew that since he was the last person who'd worked on it, he could be in serious trouble if a fault turned out to have caused Mr. Luckit's death. And it was at that moment that Sam realized he couldn't hide and hope not to get caught. Deep down, he knew that he was going to have to do the right thing.

***

The front door was open, and as Sam stopped he saw that a police officer was talking to Mrs. Luckit in the hallway. A little further beyond them, two men in overalls were just heading through to the utility room, and Sam instinctively knew that they must be investigating the faulty boiler.

Mrs. Luckit looked over at Sam with a strangely calm expression. She was wearing no makeup, and this time her other eye was bruised and blackened.

"Can I help you, Sir?" the police officer asked.

"I, uh..."

He hesitated, and then he stepped into the hallway. He knew that he was about to effectively end his career, and that he might even end up in jail, but he also knew that he absolutely had to do the right thing.

"Sir?" the officer said after a moment.

"My name's Sam Argyle," he stammered, his voice filled with fear. "Is it true? About the boiler, I mean?"

"We're investigating a death," the officer replied. "Did you know the deceased, Jacob Luckit?"

"I did, sort of," Sam said, looking at Mrs. Luckit and seeing that calm expression still on her face. He knew, at that moment, that she knew he must be responsible. "The thing is, a few weeks ago I..."

Again, his voice trailed off.

"You *what*, Sir?" the officer asked.

"I, uh..." He paused, and then he took a deep breath. "A few weeks ago I came over and I did some work on the -"

"On the car," Mrs. Luckit said suddenly, interrupting him. "Yes, Sam, I remember. You came out one evening and you fixed that broken wing mirror on Jacob's car." She fixed him with a firm stare, as if she was willing him to not say anything else. "I believe Jacob phoned you a few days ago to ask if you could take another look at it, but in the circumstances I think it's better if you leave it for now. Come back another day, or don't come back at all, it's fine. I'll probably sell the car anyway, so it doesn't matter."

Confused, Sam realized that she really didn't

want him to mention that he'd worked on the boiler at all. He wanted to ask why, but for a moment he was unable to get any words out.

"What do you want us to do about all this stuff?" a voice called out from the utility room.

"Sorry," the officer said, stepping past Mrs. Luckit, "I need to go and see what they're doing. I'll be back in a moment."

Once he was gone, Sam looked at Mrs. Luckit and tried to work out what he was supposed to say. Part of him wanted to just turn around and leave, to take the opportunity she'd given him, but he knew he could never live with himself if his mistake had caused Jacob Luckit's death. He'd been working as a plumber for five years, and the thought of having perhaps killed someone was too much for him to bear.

As Mrs. Luckit made her way over to him, Sam tried to think of something to say. An apology would feel so trite and empty, but he figured it was the only way to start.

"I'm sorry," she said suddenly. "You should go now."

"I -"

"You should go," she said again, more firmly this time. A moment later, she put a hand on his arm. "I've got everything handled. I told Jacob so many times that he should have that old boiler fixed, but he never listened. He was always trying to save a few pennies."

"Mrs. Luckit, I -"

"I'm just so relieved that Dean and I were at my parents' house," she added. "It was the first time in years that the two of us have gone to see them like that. Jacob wasn't particularly happy about it, but I managed to persuade him. The funny thing is, there was a little voice in the back of my head, telling me that this weekend I should really make sure to take Dean out of the house for a few days. I was in the utility room with Jacob, he was... Well, it doesn't matter what he was doing, not now. But I heard that voice, it told me it had everything under control, and that all I had to do was take Dean away for the weekend."

Sam stared at her, and he began to realize that she was talking about the same voice that he'd heard.

"Everything's going to be just fine," she explained. "No-one did anything wrong. The boiler worked perfectly after you fixed it. It worked perfectly every time you fixed it. I guess, if something *wants* to break, you just sometimes have to let it."

Sam hesitated, not quite sure what she meant, but then the police officer stepped back into the hallway.

"Honestly," Mrs. Luckit said with a smile, "that car's probably going to be scrapped anyway.

Thank you so much for offering to fix the mirror again, Sam, but there's really no need. You did a great job. Thank you again."

She stepped back, and then she shut the door, leaving Sam standing alone on the pavement. He wanted to knock again, to ask Mrs. Luckit *exactly* what had happened, but then he realized that she seemed to have everything under control. Turning, he hurried away from the house, just as a gust of wind blew the tops of the trees and a brief rustling sound told him that everything would be okay.

***

"Martians have just landed outside and they're shooting everyone with death rays," Julie said, her voice finally rising over the din of the coffee shop. "Looks like they're about to unleash their dinosaur pets to finish up the survivors."

Looking up from his coffee, Sam stared at her for a moment with a bewildered expression.

"Oh, so you heard *that*," she added with a faint, though concerned, smile. "Earth to Sam, are you reading me? Is there something on your mind that you need to talk about?"

"No," he said quickly, perhaps too quickly. "I'm fine."

Looking down at his phone, he reread the

message his father had sent a few minutes earlier, asking him if he could help out on an emergency boiler job. The pay would be good, but Sam wasn't sure that he trusted himself anymore.

"I'm fine," he said again, mostly in an attempt to convince himself. "I'm just... tired."

Another two weeks had passed since Jacob Luckit's death, and Sam had spent much of that time in a daze. He's done a few small jobs for people here and there, but he'd turned down two boiler installations and he was fairly sure that he never wanted to touch another boiler in his life. The entire situation seemed completely unreal, and he'd still not managed to figure out exactly what he thought had happened. He knew, however, that he was slowly coming apart at the seams, and he wondered how much longer he could hide his state of mind from his girlfriend.

"Okay," she said, getting to her feet, "I need to pop next door and pick up some pants. Are you okay waiting here?"

"Sure," he murmured.

"And try to..." Her voice trailed off for a moment. "I know you're worried about something," she added finally. "Whatever it is, try to figure out how you're going to deal with it, okay?"

With that, she stepped past him. She touched his shoulder, and then her hand trailed away as she headed to the door. She cast a concerned glance back at him, and then she made her way outside.

Left alone, Sam put his head in his hands and tried to figure out how he could even begin to tell Julie what had happened. He still felt as if he had a man's death on his conscience, and in his more rational moments he realized that the whole 'talking boiler' thing couldn't possibly have really happened. Sitting back, he took a few deep breaths, and he told himself that something had to give, that he couldn't keep living this way. He'd so nearly gone to the police on a number of occasions over the past few weeks, and now he felt a tightening sense of dread in his chest as he realized that this was his only option. He'd seem crazy, he knew that; he'd probably lose everything; at least he'd be doing the right thing, however, so he began to work out exactly how he was going to make his confession.

"Hello, Sam."

Startled, he looked up and saw that Mrs. Luckit had wandered over. He hadn't even noticed that she was in the coffee shop.

"I waited until your girlfriend was gone," she said. "Was that your girlfriend? Anyway... is it okay if I sit down? Just for a moment?"

"Sure," he said, although he was in too much shock to really say anything else.

She took a seat in front of him.

"How are you keeping?" she asked.

"I..."

His voice trailed off.

"I'll cut right to it," she continued. "I had a man come and install a totally new boiler in the house. I'm going to be selling the place anyway, so it was necessary. And I had the old boiler taken away, it's probably in some landfill site by now. I don't know, whatever. That's not very environmentally friendly of me, but I don't really care right now."

"Mrs. Luckit," he said cautiously, "I -"

"Don't," she replied, putting a finger to her lips. "Don't say anything about it. We both know that what happened, can't really have happened. But it *did* happen, didn't it? I know that thing was somehow alive."

"But -"

"Again, please... don't," she said firmly. "I'm not here for a discussion. I just saw you sitting here, looking so haunted, and I wanted you to know that you're not alone. It happened to me too. Not that I can explain it, but... I guess I just don't want you to feel responsible."

Before he could even try to reply, Sam saw that Mrs. Luckit's son Dean was sitting over by a table at the far end of the shop. The poor kid, now fatherless, had his school bag on the floor, and he was staring down at his own hands as they rested in his lap. For a moment, Sam felt overcome by a profound sense of guilt. Sure, Jacob Luckit had been a monster, but that didn't change the fact that the boy had suffered a bereavement, and Sam couldn't ignore his own culpability.

"I guess there are some things we just can't understand," Mrs. Luckit said after a few seconds, her voice filled with a sense of tentative hope. "My husband used to take me into that room and beat me."

"Mrs. Luckit -"

"No, that's what he did," she continued. "There's no point dancing around the subject. And the only thing that bore witness to any of that was the boiler on the wall. Now, I can't pretend to have any idea how that *thing* came to do what it did, but I'll never stop being grateful that something – some kind of fate – intervened. Now Dean and I get to move on with our lives, and we're going to do that a long way from here. I just hope you can get past what happened. It wasn't your fault, you know."

He opened his mouth to reply to her, but then he realized that he didn't quite know what to say. Accepting that some kind of sentient boiler had caused the accident, that the boiler had been responsible, just seemed like the easy way out.

"We have to go," Mrs. Luckit added, checking her watch. "We're actually leaving town today. I'm glad I saw you though, Sam. And thank you. I hope everything works out."

She gestured for her son, who climbed off

his seat and began gathering his belongings.

"Come on, Dean!" Mrs. Luckit called out as she hurried on ahead to the door. "We're going to be late!"

Sam watched as Dean trudged across the coffee shop. The boy looked so tired, as if his backpack was filled with bricks, and Sam couldn't help but think that most of that weight probably came from a sense of profound sorrow. A moment later, however, Dean adjusted his backpack, and the top fell open, allowing an old, heavy book to fall out and thud to the floor. The book skittered across the tiles for a moment, before coming to a rest next to Sam's chair.

Leaning down, he picked the book up. He held it out to Dean, and that's when he spotted the title 'How to Summon Demons' printed in gold lettering on the book's red cloth cover.

He looked up at Dean, and they made eye contact for a moment before the boy snatched the book and hurried out of the coffee shop. As he left, he brushed past Julie, who was returning with a bag from the shop next door.

"Everything alright in here?" she asked as she retook her seat opposite Sam. "Sorry I was gone a little longer than I expected, I got stuck in the queue behind this woman who just took forever to do everything."

"It's fine," Sam said, glancing out the

window and watching as Dean walked away. The boy looked back at him for a moment before disappearing from view.

For a moment, Sam was struck by the sadness of Dean's expression, as if the kid was afflicted by some kind of horror that filled him with fear. Although he tried to focus on the thought that he was just imagining things, Sam still couldn't quite shake the feeling that Dean Luckit was terrified by something.

"So I was thinking," Julie continued, "that we could try to do something this afternoon to take our minds off everything. We could go for a walk, maybe find a pub out in the countryside, just get out of town." She paused, watching his expression carefully, hoping to spot some sign that she'd found a way to lift his mood. "A change of scenery can really do wonders," she added, "and we could get something to eat, maybe have a drink or two, just decompress and -"

"Actually, I have a job to get to," he said suddenly, interrupting her.

"A job?"

"Dad asked if I could help out on a boiler installation," he continued, and then he paused for a moment, as he realized that he had to make a choice. Was he going to get back on the horse and work again, or was he going to hide away forever? "I don't know," he added, as he felt a familiar sense of fear in his chest. "I just don't know..."

***

Sitting in the back of his mother's car, Dean Luckit stared down at the book on his lap. As the car rumbled over a bump in the road, Dean tried to ignore the sound of the radio station, and he began to hear a faint whispering sound coming from the book. He told himself that he was wrong, that the sound couldn't be real, but slowly the voice became louder and more insistent.

"Okay," the book whispered, "I gave you what you asked for. Now it's time for you to pay me back."

SITCOM

Everybody laughs.

The look on Dad's face is priceless. Mom accidentally dumped the entire pot of pasta sauce on his lap, right after he finally got his new white suit back from the store. He's been fussing about that suit all week, he even took on an extra part-time job as a car washer at the mall so he could earn some extra bucks, and now it's completely ruined. All that work, all that effort, and once again Dad looks like a chump. Sometimes I feel sorry for him, but never for long; his humiliations are always so funny, and he always bounces right back.

"You know," he says after a moment, "sometimes I think I'm the unluckiest man in all of Litchford."

"When *don't* you think you're the unluckiest man in all of Litchford?" my brother Mickey asks after a pause, raising a skeptical eyebrow.

Again, everybody laughs, and my oh-so-precocious brother returns his attention to his dinner.

"Mickey, don't be mean to your father," Mom says, as she grabs a napkin and tries to wipe the sauce away. In doing so, she only succeeds in smearing it all across Dad's chest.

The laughter rumbles on.

"So, Phil," Grandma says, with a mischievous glint in her eyes, "would now be a good time to talk about you taking another look at my lawnmower?"

The laughter erupts as Dad turns and glares at her.

I open my mouth to say something, but then I hesitate. I haven't spoken for a while, in fact I've been very much in the background for this whole week, and I just feel as if I don't have anything funny to say. As the laughter continues, I try really hard to think of something, but it's almost as if my mind is blank. All I can come up with, at most, is a few really lame one-liners. In this family, if you don't have anything funny to say, you kind of get ignored, and I haven't had anything funny to say for quite a while. Sometimes I feel as if I'm fading into the background.

"Hey, Dad," I manage finally, "you look like you lost an argument in a jam factory."

As soon as those words have left my lips, I know I shouldn't have bothered. Still, the laughter continues, getting louder and louder as we all stare at Dad's discomfort. He looks so totally frustrated, and I honestly feel like this is the perfect culmination to the saga of his white suit. Hopefully he'll get rid of it now and we'll never hear it mentioned again, and then next week we can get on with something else entirely. That's always how things work around here in the end.

Somewhere in the distance, jaunty music is playing. Did someone leave the radio on upstairs again?

***

Opening my eyes, I find myself staring up at the darkness of my bedroom ceiling. I blink a couple of times, not really understand what's happening, and then I sit up in bed. The whole house is completely silent, and I can't even hear Dad snoring. He *did* snore once, last year, for about a week, but now there's no sound at all. I sit and listen, waiting for something to happen, but I guess everyone else is fast asleep.

I've never, in all my life, woken up in the middle of the night. To be honest, I didn't even think it was possible.

As I climb out of bed, I look at the clock on

the nightstand and see that it's exactly 3am. Every single night, I get into bed at 10pm and I close my eyes, and then I wake up feeling refreshed and raring to go at 7am. I'm sixteen years old, and my life is pretty much on rails. Nothing really changes from one week to the next. Now, standing in my dark bedroom, I feel wide awake and I'm struggling to figure out what I should do next. I guess I ought to just get back into bed and try to go to sleep again, although I can't help wondering what it's like downstairs right now.

I hesitate, and then I creep to the door and pull it open.

There's nobody out on the landing. Mom and Dad's bedroom door is ajar, but I still don't hear any snoring. I wait, just in case someone else is up, and then I make my way over to the top of the stairs. Looking down, I see that the hallway is completely dark, so that means I'm the only one who's awake. Again, I know full well that I should go back to bed, that I have no right to be up and about this late, but I can't ignore the sense of curiosity in my chest. The more I stare down into the darkness below, the more I want to go down there and take a look for myself. After all, who knows whether I'll ever get another chance?

This must be the longest I've ever gone without hearing laughter.

I glance back at Mom and Dad's door again,

and then I start slowly and quietly picking my way downstairs. This feels really wrong, as if I'm breaking about a million rules, but I just can't stop myself. I've never broken a rule before in my life, I've always been the conscientious member of the family, almost to a fault. In fact, I've sometimes worried that I'm slightly boring. As I reach the hallway downstairs, however, I feel a strange kind of flickering anticipation in my chest, almost as if I'm alive for the first time ever.

I listen to the house.

All I hear is silence.

I look around, and then I creep through to the front room. The floorboards creak a little beneath my steps, and I wince as I worry that perhaps I'll wake the others. Coming down here still feels so naughty, and then as I stop and look over at the sofa I can't help thinking that the house looks so different now. There's just enough light coming through the window for me to see the empty sofa, and I'm struck by how different everything looks. Usually the front room is the focus of all the activity in the house, but right now I almost feel as if I'm in a tomb. The ever-present laughter is missing, and that sends a shiver down my spine.

Spotting a cushion that's been left out of place, I wander over and set it right. As I do that, however, I'm suddenly struck by the sense that I'm being watched. I look around, worried that one of the others has come down to see what I'm doing, but all I see is the emptiness of the room. I find it so strange to see all the shadows, but then I have to remind myself that in the seven years since we moved into this house, I've never once been down here at night. Funny, huh?

Still feeling as if I'm being watched, I look around at all the walls, but there's still nothing. I force myself to head toward the door that leads into the kitchen. I tell myself that I'm *not* being watched, that of course I'm imagining the whole thing, but then I stop in the doorway as I hear the faintest rustle of movement somewhere nearby. I freeze, looking through at the darkened kitchen and at the empty seats around the table, and then I hear the rustling sound again.

Making my way to the sink, I grab a glass and start pouring myself some water, except suddenly the faucet doesn't work. I try a couple more times, but no water comes out, and I furrow my brow as I realize that somehow the supply must be temporarily cut off.

And then I hear the rustling sound again.

This time, I turn and look to my left, and I realize that the sound seems to be coming from the far end of the front room. Except, as I look across the room, I realize that I can't *see* the far end at all. It's almost as if the front room only has three walls. I tell myself that this is foolish, of course, and that obviously the fourth wall is out there in the darkness, but then I try to remember what that wall looks like and I draw a blank. Squinting, I try to see through the darkness, but it's as if the far end of the wall is just a huge, empty void.

I hear the rustling sound again, and now I'm more convinced than ever that I'm being watched. Something out there, beyond the fourth wall, is staring at me.

I open my mouth to call out, but then I stop myself.

This is crazy.

I'm letting my imagination run wild.

Still, I'm unable to stop staring back at the void, and every few seconds I hear another sound. A click here, a rustle there, and then finally what sounds like somebody clearing their throat. My first thought is that we might have a burglar in the house, but then I remind myself that we had a burglar last year and nothing *ever* happens twice around here. Besides, that burglar turned out to be Dad's boss, and the whole misunderstanding was quickly sorted out. In fact, nobody talks about it anymore.

I step forward, making my way toward the fourth wall, even though the darkness persists. I know that the wall has to come into view at some point soon, but it remains stubbornly absent until finally I reach the edge of the kitchen and see that there's nothing beyond.

After hesitating for a moment, I hold my hands out and reach into the void, and I feel an icy coldness hanging in the air. It's almost as if I've reached the end of the world, and when I look down I see that the kitchen floor just kind of stops just a short distance ahead of my feet.

I look over my shoulder and see the kitchen table, and in that moment I realize that I've never been this far away from the other side of the room.

Suddenly I hear a cough, and I turn to look back out into the void.

"Hello?" I call out, before I have a chance to stop myself.

I wait, but now all I hear is silence.

Looking down at my feet again, I tell myself that I have to be brave and step forward, but I can't quite bring myself to do that. I can't shake the fear that I'll simply topple over and plummet into an endless fall, even though I know that something like that is impossible.

I take a deep breath, and then – just as I'm about to turn and walk away – I see that there's something just ahead in the darkness.

Crouching down, I squint and try to get a better look, and I finally realize that I can see some sort of cable running past. That, at least, suggests that there must be some kind of floor, so I reach down and sure enough my hand quickly presses against a cold, dusty set of tiles. I look up again, and somehow my eyes are adjusting to the darkness now and I realize I can see what looks like several large cameras towering above me.

Getting to my feet, I cautiously step toward the cameras, which are all pointing into our kitchen. I make my way past them, and then I realize that a little further off I can see rows of empty seats rising high up from the ground. It's as if there's room here for some kind of theater audience, and if these seats were filled there'd be hundreds of people staring directly at our family's kitchen. Turning, I realize that they'd actually have a great view of our entire house, and a shudder passes through my chest

Hearing another rustling sound, this time from somewhere off to the left, I turn and look up toward the very highest row of seats, all the way at the back.

"Hello?" I say again, and now my voice is echoing slightly in this huge space. "Is anybody there?"

I wait a moment, and then I take a couple of steps forward until I almost trip on the bottom of a set of steps. I take a few seconds to adjust my balance, and then I step forward again.

"Stop!" a voice hisses from somewhere high up. "Don't wake them!"

I freeze, horrified by the thought that someone *is* in our house. Then again, as I look around at the rows of empty seats, I'm starting to realize that somehow I seem to have left the house.

"They're asleep," the voice continues, "but it doesn't take much to wake them. Please, I'm begging you, let them rest."

I open my mouth to ask who he means, but at the same time I realize I can sense somebody nearby. I look around, and again I only see the rows of empty seats, but it's almost as if there are lots of invisible people sitting here. That's not possible, of course, but the sensation only get stronger as I start making my way up the set of shallow steps that runs between the aisles.

"Stop!" the voice in the distance yells, and this time I'm just about able to spot a figure scurrying along behind the top row of seats.

Whoever this person is, he seems to be on his hands and knees.

"What's going on?" I ask, quickening my pace. "What are you doing in my family's house? What are all these seats doing here?"

I quickly reach the top of the steps, just as a boy crawls into view and gets to his feet. Clearly startled, he stares at me with a horrified expression, and I see that he's roughly my own age, maybe slightly younger, and he's wearing rough, tattered clothing.

"Who are you?" I whisper.

"You're *her*," he replies.

"What are you talking about?"

He takes a step back, and then he looks past me, as if something nearby is filling him with terror.

"I won't ask you again," I say firmly, and more loudly this time, "who -"

"Quiet!" he hisses, holding a finger up against his lips. "Please, I don't know exactly what'll happen if you wake them, but I don't think it'll be good."

"If I wake *who*?" I ask, and now I'm starting to lose my temper. "Okay, whatever, you can explain it to the police when they get here, because that's who I'm calling!"

"No!" he gasps, as I turn to go back down the steps.

Suddenly I freeze as I see that the seats are all now full, and I look around to see the backs of hundreds of heads all staring down toward the distant, dimly-lit kitchen. I take a step back, not quite believing what I'm seeing, and then the boy grabs my arm and pulls me back even further.

"They're sleeping," he whispers. "I think that might be a very good thing."

Turning to him, I realize that this entire situation makes no sense whatsoever.

"We have to get out of here," he continues. "I tried, but the staff locked the doors when they left for the night. I never should have stayed!"

"What staff?" I ask, struggling to stay calm.

"I don't know who you are, but you're trespassing in our house!"

"Don't make too much noise," he tells me. "I almost woke one of them up earlier, I saw his eyes starting to open, but then I stayed really quiet and he went back to sleep. We might not be so lucky the next time."

"Where did all these people come from?" I reply, as I think back to the empty seats I saw on the way up here. "This doesn't make any sense."

I pull away from the boy and start making my way down the steps, but then I stop as I realize that I can no longer see the people on the back row of seats. I head up the steps, and now I see those people again, as if they reappeared in the blink of an eye.

"You can only see them from behind, I think," the boy says. "That kind of seems logical, in a way. At least as far as *anything* in this place is logical."

"Is this some kind of optical illusion?" I ask, stepping down the steps and then back up several times, and watching as the people flicker in an out of view. "Okay, that's kind of cool, but it's also kind of creepy." I turn to the boy again. "And it also doesn't explain who you are and what you're doing in this... weird... strange part of the house that I never even noticed before."

"If you could see them from the front," he

replies, "then you might have noticed them before."

"What are you talking about?" I snap.

"Quiet!" he hisses, grabbing me again and pulling me close.

"Will you quite doing that?" I reply.

"My name's Tom," he explains, keeping his voice low. "I'm..." He pauses for a moment, as I begin to notice a slightly fusty smell in the air. "I don't exactly have anywhere to live," he continues finally.

"You're homeless?"

"I guess that's the word for it," he replies. "My family... I don't really want to talk about it, but the thing is, I managed to sneak into this studio tonight and I thought I could hide away until everyone went home, and then I'd be able to spend the night somewhere at least slightly warm. I was doing pretty good, too, I was actually starting to feel like I'd done something smart for once. And then..."

His voice trails off.

"Then I noticed *them*," he adds.

"What studio?" I ask, still not managing to get my head around what he's telling me.

"So why are you here?" he replies. "You're, like, a star. Why are you hanging around here all by yourself after everyone else has gone home?"

"I literally do not have a clue what you're talking about," I tell him. "This is my home, I live here. I went to bed, and then I came downstairs because I couldn't sleep and that's when I found you here. That's just the facts of what happened, so really you're the one who has to do the explaining before I call the cops!"

Filled with horror, I take a step back.

"Wait," I stammer, "are you here to murder me?"

"What?" He sighs. "Don't make so much noise! I already warned you!"

"My dad has a gun," I continue, backing away a little further, "and -"

Suddenly I bump against one of the seats, and I freeze as I hear a faint, snarling growl coming from right over my shoulder. I wait, as the growl continues to slowly rumble, and then I slowly turn and see that the figure in the seat is starting to shudder slightly. Now that I'm close, I can tell that the back of the figure's head is somehow concave, as if it's been scooped and hollowed out, and I can see open gaps where there should be the backs of the eyes and the mouth. The mouth gap is moving, almost as if it's letting out a slow mumble, and a moment later I realize that the inside of the figure's head is linked with what looks like glistening black veins that thread in and out of gray, cracked flesh.

"Get away from it," Tom says, grabbing my hand and pulling me away from the seats. "Damn it, if you've woken one of them up..."

"What is that thing?" I ask, as the figure

continues to twitch in its seat. "What are you all doing in my house?"

Before Tom can answer, the figure falls still, although I realize after a few seconds that it's still letting out a low grumble.

"I meant what I said earlier," I continue, turning to Tom, "my dad -"

"Hell!" he snaps, his eyes widening with shock as he takes another step back.

I turn to look at the seat again, and to my horror I see that the figure is slowly starting to get to its feet. As it does so, it seems to be waking some of the others figures, several of which are starting to twitch now.

"This way!"

Squeezing my hand tight, Tom drags me along the aisle at the back of the seats. I'm too shocked to stop him, so we run toward a set of double doors and I let him pull me through. At the last moment, I look back and – as the doors swing shut – I see that about a dozen of the figures are standing now. One of them turns, as if to look this way, but once he's facing me I realize that I can no longer see him.

And then the doors swing shut.

"We have to get out of here," Tom tells me.

He starts pulling me along the brightly-lit corridor, but I pull my hand away from him and stop.

"What are you doing?" he hisses. "Move!"

"What is this place?" I ask, looking around and seeing that the walls are lined with posters for various TV shows I've never heard of. "How is this place connected to my house?"

"Are you high?" Tom replies. "Is that it? Are you on some kind of Hollywood drug trip?"

"Hollywood? What are you talking about?"

"I always heard actors were weird," he continues, "but you're out of your mind. Whatever those things are, we can figure it out later, but right now we need to find the exit. Come on, we have to keep moving!"

He reaches out to grab my hand again, but this time I pull away.

"I'm not going anywhere with you," I say firmly, trying to hide the fact that I'm struggling to hold back tears. I'm scared, and I just want to go home. "You have to leave, do you understand?"

"Tanya, I'm serious," he replies, looking past me toward the set of double doors. "We can talk when we're outside, after we've called for help but right now -"

"My name's not Tanya," I say, interrupting him.

"What do you mean?"

"My name's Jill," I tell him. "Jill Cooper. And if you -"

"How high *are* you?" he asks. "Seriously?

Are you so out of your mind that you actually think you're your character?"

"What are you -"

Stopping myself just in time, I realize that there's absolutely no point arguing with this guy. He's plainly nuts, and I figure I need to go home and wake Dad up so that he can chase this complete moron out of the house. I start backing away, and then I turn to head back the way we just came.

Suddenly the double doors begin to creak open.

I stop, and I watch as the doors are slowly pushed aside. There's nobody there, but a moment later I realize I can hear footsteps squeaking against the shiny, polished floor.

"They're coming!" Tom yells, grabbing my hand again and this time forcing me to follow him.

I let him lead me along the corridor, but I can't help looking over my shoulder and watching as the doors remain open. It's as if several invisible figures are coming through into the corridor, but I know that's completely impossible.

A moment later, we stop at another door, but when Tom tries the handle he finds that it's locked.

"Security must have closed the place up for the night," he says, turning to me. He looks along the corridor, and when I follow his gaze I see that the double doors at the far end are finally swinging shut.

"I can hear footsteps," I whisper, as the squeaks slowly come closer.

"Through here!" Tom yells, pulling me through another door, which he then slams shut.

Startled, I step back and watch as he drags a desk across the door to keep it shut, and then I turn to see that we're in some kind of office. There's a long table in the middle of the room, with several seats all around, and over on the far wall there's a large whiteboard with lots of scribbled notes in different colors. I step over to take a closer look, and I quickly notice several words and phrases that seem familiar somehow.

"Phil buys a motor-home," I read out loud. "Phil goes duck hunting. Phil enters a chili-eating contest."

Looking across the board, I see more suggestions.

"Maggie meets an old flame from high school," I read. "Mickey fights a boy at school for a hat."

Making my way around the table, I spot a column with the name Jill at the top, and nothing but questions marks underneath.

"This must be the writers' room," Tom says, as he comes over to join me. "I've seen documentaries about how these shows are made. During the day, they get a bunch of writers to sit around and come up with ideas for episodes." He stops and looks at the board for a moment. "I guess the rumors were true, huh? They're really struggling to figure out what to do with your character. Is that why everyone says you're leaving, or is it the drug problem? Or is it that dirt-bag guy all the tabloids say you're dating?"

I look over at him.

"I don't read that shit," he adds. "I just heard about it, that's all."

"I don't know what you're talking about," I reply cautiously, "but I want to go home. Right now."

"We need to find a phone and call for help," he says. "You don't happen to have your phone on you, do you?"

"It's in my room," I tell him, "but none of this makes any -"

Before I can finish, we both hear a loud banging sound, and we turn to see that someone's trying to open the door from out in the corridor. I watch as the handle turns several times, but it's getting caught on the desk and even after a series of thuds the door refuses to open.

"That'll hold them for now," Tom says, "but they're gonna find a way in eventually."

He looks the other way.

"Probably through there," he adds.

Following his gaze, I see a long glass window on the other side of the room, looking through into some kind of open plan office.

"There has to be a phone somewhere," he continues, hurrying past me and starting to search the room as the knocks continue on the door. "What kind of workplace doesn't have a phone?"

"This is like a production office for a TV show," I whisper, as I feel a shiver pass down my spine. Stepping over to the desk, I look down and see several magazines, one of which has a cover photograph of my family. Reaching down, I pick the magazine up and try to figure out exactly what's happening here. "Is *Litchford Life* turning sour?" I read from the headline. "Eight seasons in, TV's hottest comedy faces a make-or-break challenge."

"Why is there no goddamn phone?" Tom shouts angrily, his voice filled with panic.

I start flicking through the magazine, and I soon find more photos of my family. I'm starting to feel as if I must be losing my mind, or that I might be dreaming, because nothing that I'm seeing right now is making any kind of sense at all. This magazine has loads and loads of pictures of me and Mom and Dad and Mickey, and Grandma and our neighbors and a whole bunch of other people we know, but they're talking about us as if we have these other names that don't make any sense. It's almost as if they think we're characters in some kind of TV sitcom.

And then, turning to another page, I see a

photo of myself.

Except... it's not me.

It *can't* be me.

This photo shows someone who looks a lot like me, but she's clearly drunk and out of her mind on drugs. She's stepping out of a car late at night, with some scraggy looking guy clinging to her, and it's look like lots of photographers are trying to get shots of the pair of them. Her clothes are almost falling off her, and she looks as if she's in the process of stumbling. When I look down at the text at the bottom of the picture, I see that the photo is supposed to show someone named Tanya Simmonds, who was caught partying late in Hollywood.

This is starting to get really creepy.

"They have a TV, but no phone," Tom mutters, and I turn to see that he's grabbed a remote control, which he uses to switch the TV on. "Do you think it's possible to get Zoom or something up and running on this thing?"

"To get *what* up and running?" I ask, feeling a little light-headed.

A moment later, realizing that the banging has stopped on the other side of the door, I take a couple of steps back while still holding the magazine. Whatever was out there in that corridor, it seems to be gone now, and I'm tempted to pull the desk aside and race back out there. I don't know what's going on, but I figure I can be back in the house inside of maybe ninety seconds, if I run really fast, and then I can wake everybody up and get them to help me figure out what's going on here.

I take a step forward and reach out to move the desk.

In an instant, the TV comes to life, and I turn to see that Tom is flicking from channel to channel. He seems distracted, which makes this the perfect time to get out of here, but at the same time I can't help worrying that there still might be something dangerous out there in the corridor. I don't hear anything, but that just makes me worry that those *things* might be lurking out there and getting ready to attack as soon as I open the door.

"Just wake up," I whisper, before reaching up and pinching the side of my neck, hoping that the pain will jerk me out of this nightmare. "Wake up and all of this will be -"

"It's you!" Tom says suddenly.

Turning, I see that he's still staring at the TV. He's got some sleazy tabloid news show running, and after a moment I realize I can see of a girl stumbling out of some bar. She's wearing really skimpy clothing, she's clearly wasted, and as she stops and starts vomiting all over the sidewalk I catch a proper glimpse of her face.

She's me.

At least, she looks like me.

I glance down at the magazine again, and I swear I feel as if my mind is about to implode.

"- are still refusing to confirm or deny reports that the star has checked into rehab," a voice on the TV says as Tom turns the volume up. "It's now been over a week since the popular *Litchford Life* star has been seen in public, and the timing of her disappearance couldn't be worse, with rumors swirling that spiraling wage demands are about to see her written out of the show that made her a household name."

"Who's that?" I ask, stepping closer to the TV.

The image changes and I see what appears to be a clip from my life. I see myself talking to Dad, sitting on the sofa with him. I'm wearing my favorite baseball shirt.

"While she plays a holier-than-thou girl next door in the hit sitcom," the newscaster continues, "Tanya Simmonds seems to be unraveling off the screen. A decision about her participation in the ninth season is said to be imminent, but we're hearing off the record reports that the character of Jill Cooper might be missing when the show returns. Some rumors even suggest that a recast is being considered."

"No way," Tom says, turning to me. "They'd never recast you. If they didn't do it to those Olsen sisters, they wouldn't do it to you. I'm calling that one right now."

"What the hell are you on about?" I ask, unable to take my eyes off the screen as I see yet more video of that Tanya Simmonds girl stumbling around drunk. Finally, somehow, I force myself to turn to Tom. "I want you to tell me what's going on. Right now!"

"I have no idea," he replies. "Those things out there are -"

"I want to know what's going on with me!" I scream, grabbing him by the shoulders and slamming him against the wall as I feel my rage and panic starting to boil over. Tears are running down my face now. "I want to know where I am!"

"I guess we're backstage," he stammers. "I told you, I crept into the place tonight. I hid and watched the taping of another episode of that show and then -"

"What show?" I shout.

"It was about your dad getting a new white suit," he explains. "It was pretty lame, even by sitcom standards. And then -"

"My life is not a sitcom!" I hiss.

"No, it's a train wreck," he replies. "Look at you, you must be worth millions, and you're running around like a lunatic." He pauses for a moment, and I swear it's almost as if he pities me. "I guess it's true what they say," he adds finally. "Child stars have it rough. I mean, you must have been, what, eight years old when this show began?"

"There's no show," I tell him, as I feel my head starting to spin.

Letting go of Tom, I step back, only to bump against the table. I feel as if I'm about to faint, but I somehow manage to hold myself up.

"You're really into this, aren't you?" Tom says after a few seconds. "Is it the drugs? Are you suffering from some kind of psychosis?"

"I don't take drugs," I reply.

"Apart from that episode where you accidentally got high," he says.

"My neighbor once put some pot in a cookie batch," I tell him, "but..."

Stopping suddenly, I realize that there's no way he should know about that. It happened ages ago, maybe two years back, but we made sure nobody found out. Sure, it might have been a little funny when I was high as a kite, but I'd have been mortified if anyone had seen me in that state.

"You really think you're Jill Cooper, don't you?" Tom says, and then he allows himself a faint smile. "Man, you picked the wrong night to have an identity crisis. So what drugs are you on, anyway? Speed? Acid? Some kind of mix?"

"Is this a prank?" I ask, still trying to get things straight in my head. "Did my stupid little brother put you up to this?"

"So where do your people think you are

right now?" he replies. "Do they actually think you're in rehab? 'Cause they're gonna get quite a shock when they find out that you're here. Don't worry, though, I won't tip the media off. You look like you've already been through enough."

"I want to go home," I tell him.

"If you're in rehab, you might have to be -"

"I want to go home!" I yell, and now more tears are running down my face. "I want to go back to bed and pretend none of this is happening, and in the morning I want to get up and see Mom and Dad again and Grandma, and even Mickey!"

"You're out of your mind," he says, shaking his head in a state of absolute disbelief. "I think this is actually serious, isn't it? Like, you need proper medical help."

I open my mouth to tell him that he's wrong, but then I realize that he might actually have a point. I feel like I'm losing my grip on reality, and I have no idea what I'm supposed to do next. I look around, hoping against hope that Mom or Dad might suddenly appear and make everything okay, but of course there's no sign of them.

"I want to go home," I sob again, and this time I feel myself starting to break down into wave after wave of tears. Putting my hands over my face, I start gulping for air. "Why can't I just go home?"

"Easy," Tom says, stepping over to me and putting a hand on my shoulder. "I'm gonna get you home, okay?"

I look up at him through the tears.

"I promise," he continues, squeezing my shoulder slightly. "We're gonna get away from those things, whatever they are, and we're gonna get you the help that you need. And I won't even sell my story after, how's that? Your mental health issues should be private."

"I just want to go home," I whimper. "Back to the house."

"You know going home means leaving the studio, right?" he says. "Can you cling on to that fact for me?"

"But my home is -"

"It's really important," he adds, interrupting me. "Your name is Tanya Simmonds and -"

"No!" I blurt out.

"It is," he says firmly. "Really, you have to trust me on this. Your name is Tanya Simmonds and you're an actress on a sitcom called *Litchford Life*, and you're obviously having a pretty major wobble. But I'm sure you'll be fine, just as soon as you've seen some doctors and you've got whatever medication you need. You seem to be convinced that you're your character from the show, but you're not her. You're Tanya." He pauses, and then he offers a faint smile. "You're actually a pretty major star," he adds, "which is kinda cool. For you, I mean. You're loaded, and you've got a bright future ahead if you can just kick this tough time. I wouldn't record another album, though. That one you released last year was rough."

"Album?" I reply, and now my voice is trembling.

"Sorry, that was mean of me," he says. "Kind of a low shot."

I want to tell him that none of this makes sense, but I just can't get the words out? What if I really *am* going crazy? I remember my life, and I'm not willing to accept that I have false memories, but I guess it's possible that I might be a little... confused. After all, I can't deny that I just came out of my house and found myself in some kind of theater or auditorium, and now I'm backstage at a TV studio. Every time I open my mouth to tell Tom that he must be wrong, I realize that I'll just sound even more nuts.

Suddenly something slams against the door, and we both turn to see it shudder in its frame. Seconds later there's a second, heavier impact, and I turn to look back at Tom.

"We need to get out of here," he tells me. "That's our first job."

I watch as he heads over to the window, and he starts trying to find some way to get it open. Figuring that I should help, I go over to the other end, even as the pounding on the door becomes stronger and stronger. A moment later, I hear a splitting sound. When I glance back across the room, I see that the door seems to be buckling slightly.

"They're going to break through soon if they keep that up," I point out.

"Why doesn't this damn thing open?" Tom mutters, before stopping and looking over at the chairs. "Looks like there's only one way out of here."

He hurries over and grabs the nearest chair, and then he turns and slams it into the window. To my surprise, the chair merely bounces off the glass, with such force that it flies out of Tom's hands and hits the table.

"What is that thing, bulletproof?" Tom says, grabbing another chair and turning around to try again. "I'll aim for the corners. The corners are always weak, right?"

"We have to hurry," I point out, taking one of the other chairs so that I can lend a hand. "Whatever those things are, I don't want to be here when they get into the room."

Without answering, Tom slams the chair into the window again, and again, and I join him after a moment. We batter the window with the chairs, but we're still not able to break through, and finally I stop as I hear another splitting sound. Turning, I'm horrified to see that the door has been almost broken down the middle, and a second later there's another loud crunch as the head of an ax is sent smashing through the wood.

"We're running out of time!" I tell Tom. "I think -"

Before I can finish, the ax smashes the door out of the frame, sending the two sides crashing to the ground. As soon as I spot a figure standing out in the corridor, I scream and throw the chair, hitting the figure with such force that it stumbles back. I grab another chair and throw that as well, as I feel a sense of panic bursting through my body.

"Hurry!" I yell to Tom, as I throw more chairs. "I can't hold them back for much longer!"

Grabbing the last chair, I throw it at the door. I start looking around for something else I can throw, but then I hear a loud groan and I turn just as one of the chairs is sent hurtling back toward me. I raise my hands to protect my face, but the chair slams into me with enough force to knock me over and send me thudding down to the ground.

"Tom!" I shout. "What -"

"Will someone stop throwing chairs at me?" a voice screams, and I turn to see a figure stumbling through the open doorway, carrying what appears to be a bottle of vodka. "Are you people out of your goddamn minds?"

I open my mouth to yell at Tom, but then I freeze as I realize that I recognize the figure.

Tossing the ax aside, she steps past the

remains of the door and then stops to take a long swig from her bottle. I see tracks of vodka dribbling down her chin, and then she lets out a gasp as she lowers the bottle and looks directly at me. Her hair's a mess, her eyes are reddened and she looks like she's been dragged through a hedge, but I can't deny the fact that I'm staring at the same girl I saw just a few minutes ago on the news.

It's me.

I mean, it's her.

It's Tanya Simmonds.

She lets out a burp, and then she wipes her chin.

"What the hell's going on in here?" she asks, taking a couple of steps forward. "Great, are you my replacement? I never thought they'd actually have the balls to go for a recast, but I've gotta admit, you look pretty good." She tilts her head slightly. "If I didn't know better, I think I'd almost believe that you're me."

"What?" I stammer, unable to believe what I'm seeing. "Who... I mean... how... I..."

"We're identical," she points out, before reaching up and touching the large silver ring piercing in the septum of her nose. "Well, apart from this. The assholes on the show always make me take it out for filming, they don't think prissy little Jill would get one of these bad boys."

"You've got to be kidding me," Tom says as

he comes over and helps me up from the floor.

"There's no rehab facility in the world that can hold me," the girl says proudly, before taking another drink. "I don't know what planet they think they're on, but I have my ways of getting out. And I'm not going back, either. I don't need rehab, so why should I let them lock me away?" She shuffles past us, and we both turn to watch as she sets the bottle down and wanders over to take a look at the whiteboard. "I don't have a problem," she adds. "They *want* me to have a problem, so they can take over my life and my finances and milk me more than they've ever milked me before, but there's no way I'm letting that happen."

She stares at the board for a moment, before grabbing a marker pen from the side.

"How can they say they're out of ideas for my character?" she asks, as she starts writing some suggestions in the 'Jill' column. "I'm the real star of *Litchford Life*, everyone knows that. The only thing they should be thinking about is when they're going to cancel this miserable pile of crap and give me a spin-off. Single camera this time, and on cable so we can make it properly realistic. That's the way of the future."

She throws the marker aside and turns to look at us.

"Spill, then," she adds. "Come on, one of you has to tell me what's going on here. And let me remind you, I have a contract."

"I don't get it," Tom says, taking a step toward her. "If you're Tanya Simmonds, then..."

He pauses, before turning to me.

"Then who are *you*?" he asks.

"I told you," I reply, feeling more confused than ever, "my name is Jill Cooper and -"

"No, I'm Jill Cooper!" Tanya roars, as she points at her own chest. "Never forget that, okay? No-one else can play that dumb bitch! I am now, and always will be, the only Jill Cooper!"

She looks me up and down, and I can see the disdain in her expression.

"And who the hell are you, bitch?" she adds.

"I..."

My voice trails off, and it takes me a moment before I actually remember the answer.

"My name is Jill Cooper," I stammer, "and -"

"I warned you!" she snaps, storming toward me, only for Tom to step in the way and push her back. "Let me at that little faker!" she yells. "Do you seriously think you can take my place, bitch? What did they do, give you surgery to make you look like me? Is that it? I hope they paid you upfront, because you're never going anywhere near that sound stage! You're nothing!"

Stepping back, horrified by the venom in her voice, I feel for a moment as if I just want to run and hide.

"Calm down!" Tom tells her, before shoving her back toward the whiteboard. "We don't know what's going on here, okay? If you can just stop yelling for a minute, we might actually be able to figure things out." He turns to me. "Okay," he continues, "so you're not Tanya Simmonds, I can see that now. In which case, I've got to admit that she has a point. Who *are* you?"

"I'm Jill Cooper," I reply, "and -"

Tanya opens her mouth to yell at me again.

"Shut it!" Tom says, holding a finger up as he turns to her. "Just for one moment, shut your mouth and let her talk!"

Tanya rolls her eyes, but at least she stays quiet as Tom looks back at me.

"My name is... Jill Cooper," I say awkwardly, and I can hear the doubt in my own voice. "I live at 544 Horsemeadow Lane, I go to Litchford High, and I want to be a doctor when I'm older." I pause for a moment as I try to draw together some more certainties about my life. "I have a brother, he's a total brat. I'm learning to play the clarinet, although I'm not really very good at it yet, and I like painting and drawing. I want to learn to ride horses, but I've never tried it."

Again, I hesitate as I try to come up with some more suggestions.

"That's complete crap," Tanya says, crossing

her arms across her chest. "You're a terrible actress. You're nothing like Jill at all, where did the network executives find you? Have you ever taken an acting class?"

"I'm not an actor," I reply. "I've never wanted to be an actor. I don't even like being on a stage."

"What about those creatures?" Tom asks, turning to Tanya. "You were out there, did you see any sign of them?"

"Any sign of *what*?" she asks disdainfully.

Rushing past her, Tom heads out into the corridor and looks around, and then he steps back into the room.

"I think they're gone," he tells me, although he sounds a little unsure. "For now, at least. It's hard to tell, but I don't see them."

"You wouldn't, though, would you?" I point out. "Not from the front."

"What are you two maniacs talking about?" Tanya asks, as she picks up her bottle again and takes another swig. "How did you get in here, anyway? Where are the producers? I am so totally confused about what's going on here right now."

"We need to get out of here," Tom says. "How did you get into the building?"

"I have my ways."

"Tell us!"

"Bite me."

"If you don't tell us right now how you got in here," he continues, "I'll make you pay!"

"Manners, my friend," she replies with a grin. "Do you know who you're talking to? I could have security come in here and haul you out. In fact, I think that's exactly what I'll do right now."

"Do you have a phone?" I ask.

"As if," she says, rolling her eyes again. "Do you really think I'm dumb enough to carry something that'd allow me to be tracked? My dumb little friend, I'm way smarter than everyone thinks. Remember that headline last year where I was called America's favorite dumb blonde? They sure as hell got a lot wrong there."

"They won't have just given up," Tom points out.

"Sure," I reply, as I glance at the window that we so spectacularly failed to break earlier, "but how do we -"

Suddenly I spot a hint of movement, reflected in one of the monitors on a desk in the office area. I tell myself that I might be wrong, but then I see the same thing on another monitor, and that's when I realize that the strange creatures might be out there, in which case they can see us while we're standing here arguing.

"We need a plan," Tom says, taking a couple of steps back until he's almost directly in front of the window. "There's no way I'm just going to stand around here, waiting for those things to come back and get us."

"Get over here," I stammer, gesturing for him to join me as I spot more reflections. "Tom, I think they're in there."

"What?" He turns and looks at the window. "How do you -"

Before he can finish, the entire window shatters from the other side, showering this entire room with shards of glass. Tanya and I manage to pull out of the way, but Tom cries out as he drops to the ground, and when he tries to stand up I see that his face and hands have been cut to ribbons. Blood is gushing from his wounds, and he lets out a pained cry as he tries and fails to get to his feet.

Shoving Tanya out of the way, I rush forward and grab Tom, and I quickly pull him away. As I do that, shards of glass start crunching on the floor and I realize that the invisible creatures must be climbing through the broken window.

"We have to get out of here!" I yell at Tanya, who looks genuinely shocked by what she's just seen. "Run!"

I manage to get Tom out into the corridor. I try the main exit again, only to find that it's still locked, and then Tanya comes stumbling through to join us with the bottle of vodka still in her hands.

"How did you get in?" I shout. "We don't have time to mess about!"

"I..."

She hesitates, and then slowly she turns to look back into the room as invisible feet kick pieces of glass toward us. In a flash, she throws her bottle of vodka in that direction. The glass smashes, and the pieces of glass are knocked again, almost as if one of the creatures pulled back in a panic.

"This way," she says finally, turning and racing along the corridor. "Every sucker for themselves!"

"Wait!" I yell, and then I take a moment to support Tom as we limp after her. "It's going to be okay," I tell him. "We're going to get out of here, and then we're going to figure all of this out."

He tries to say something, but all he manages to get out is a few gasps.

Looking ahead, I see Tanya racing into one of the other rooms. Figuring that she at least seems to know her way around here, I force Tom to stick with me as we follow, but a moment later Tanya backs out of the room and I see that she's not alone.

"Okay, what's all this noise?" a security guard asks, before turning and spotting Tom and me. "Who the hell are these people?" He turns back to Tanya. "You said you were only coming in to fetch a few things! I never would've let you through the back door if you'd told me you had other people with you!"

"They're not with me," Tanya says

breathlessly. "They were just sort of here. Which doesn't say much for your capabilities as a guard, does it? And we both know you'd have let us in anyway. The slightest promise of getting your limp dick in my mouth, you were willing to -"

"That's enough!" he barks. "This is more than my job's worth. I want all of you to get out of here right now!"

"Fine by us!" I snap as Tom as I finally reach them.

"What happened to *him*?" the guard asks, looking down at Tom for a moment before turning to me. "Wait, who are you? You look exactly like -"

"Yeah, we know," I tell him.

"It's part of some stupid studio scheme to replace me," Tanya says. "I don't know what's going on here tonight, but someone let the loonies run free and I am *not* sticking around to find out who or why. I'm not blowing you again either, Herman, so how about you lead us out of here right now or I'll run to the tabloids and tell them all about the mean security guard who made me do bad things."

"What the hell are you -"

Before he can finish, we all hear a thudding sound from the other end of the corridor, and we turn to look back toward the broken door. A couple of pieces of wood are getting kicked out across the floor, and I immediately realize that the invisible figures are slowly but surely coming after us.

"We have to keep going," I tell the others. "They won't stop."

"What are you idiots talking about?" Herman the guard says, pushing us out of the way and stepping along the corridor, heading toward the danger. "If somebody's in there," he calls out, "you need to come out here before I make you regret your choices."

He takes a gun from a holster on his belt and aims it along the corridor.

"We don't have time for this!" I shout. "We just have to get out of here!"

"Something's coming," Herman says, and I can hear the fear in his voice. "I don't know what it is, but something's coming right this way!"

As those words leave his mouth, I see that a broken piece of wood keeps getting knocked along the corridor. Its progress is slow, but it's enough to show that sets of invisible feet are slowly making their way toward us, and after a moment I start backing away along with Tom and Tanya.

"Freeze!" Herman yells, and now he's not even sure where to aim his gun as we all hear the sound of squeaking footsteps moving closer. "I don't know what kind of trick this is, but I'm in charge of security around here and I'm telling you that there'll be consequences for any messing around!"

He's waving the gun wildly now, and it's

clear that he's lost control.

"Hey, Herman," Tanya says, "how about you stop trying to act tough, and you get your ass over to -"

Suddenly Herman screams as his right arm is yanked to one side. His gun fires before dropping to the ground, and then Herman screams again as his arm snaps in mid-air. As he spins around, his head is pulled back, and I watch in horror as blood bursts from one side of his face. The flesh is being torn away, and I watch as strings of meat are sucked up from his cheek. It's as if invisible teeth are eating into his body, and the pieces of meat are disappearing as soon as they're swallowed by the creatures.

I start to step forward, figuring that I have to help him, but Tom grabs my arm and pulls me back.

"It's too late," he stammers, barely able to get the words out. "They're eating him alive."

He's right. For a moment, I can only stare as pieces of meat are ripped from Herman's body. I can see part of his skull showing through the wounds now, and after a moment I realize that splattered blood is floating in the air, as if it's been sprayed across the otherwise invisible creatures.

"This is gross," Tanya points out. "I did a movie like this a couple of summers ago, but it's so much grosser in real life."

Herman tries to call out to us, but in that

instant his right eye socket is crushed by another heavy bite, and I watch as the eyeball is sucked out and then disappears into the mouth of one of the invisible creatures. Blood sprays from the poor man's mouth, but now he's shaking all over and after a couple more seconds he drops to his knees before finally toppling over and landing dead, flat on his face.

Dead and still.

"Why have they stopped?" I ask.

As if in answer to that question, a squeaking footsteps moves toward us, and I spot a bloodied print on the floor.

"Run!" I shout, grabbing Tom and forcing him to come with me back to the double doors at the end of the corridor. I push us through, back into the auditorium where we met earlier, and then I turn just in time to see that Tanya has come with us.

She slams the doors shut and then grabs a fire extinguisher from nearby, and she manages to wedge part of the top section between the door's handles, hopefully to keep it shut for at least a while.

"Okay," she says breathlessly, turning to us, "now what do -"

She freezes, and a moment later I turn, following her gaze and seeing the backs of all the figures that are still sitting in the seats. Sure, there are about twenty empty seats, which I guess were left by the figures that came after us, but that still leaves a few hundred of the damn things still in here with us.

"We're right back where we started," I whisper.

"What the hell is going on in here?" Tanya asks as she wanders over to join us. "What are all these -"

"Quiet!" I hiss, putting a hand over her mouth. "Trust me, you do *not* want to wake them up!"

She tries to say something, but I press my hand harder against her face, until finally she falls still. Slowly, I move my hand away, and then for a moment the three of us stare at the rows of silhouetted bodies in all the seats. The scene is surreal, almost impossible to believe, and a moment later the silence is broken by the sound of the fire extinguisher jiggling as something tries to get the door open from out in the corridor.

"They're not going to give up," I point out, looking toward the door.

"What are *they*?" Tanya asks, turning to me. "Okay, you idiots, it's time for you to level with me. Herman might have been a disgusting old bastard, but that doesn't mean I wanted to see him get eaten in front of me. Are we in some kind of reality show? Is this some trick, some way of punking me for a series?"

"It's not -"

"Hello!" she yells, looking all around. "If you think -"

"Shut up!" I snap, once again placing a hand against her mouth.

This time she struggles for a moment, but I manage to force her back against the wall and press even harder, and finally she seems to get the message.

"You have to keep your voice down!" I whisper to her. "Do you get that? Waking these things up is what got us into a mess in the first place. If we wake any more of them up, we're truly screwed."

I wait a moment, and then I slowly lower my hand.

Her lips move slightly, as if she's about to say something, but then she looks past me and for a few seconds she seems stunned by the sight of all the strange figures in the seats.

"I can't tell," she says finally, "if I need more drugs, or less drugs."

"There has to be some way out of here," Tom says, leaning against the wall. He's clearly weak from having lost so much blood. "Tanya, you got in here through the back door. How do we get there?"

"We'd have to go out the way we just came," she replies, "but it'll be locked."

"Who has the keys?"

"Well, Herman."

"Then..."

We both stare at her for a moment.

"What?" she asks cautiously.

"So we could have escaped just now?" I ask, feeling a growing sense of anger. "If that Herman guy had just listened to us, we could be out of here already?"

"Or if we'd taken the keys from his bloodied corpse," she points out. "Yeah, that would have been by far our best shot."

"I don't believe this," I say, turning away from her and putting my hands on my face as I try to keep from screaming. "All I wanted was to go to sleep and wake up and get on with my life. I was supposed to go bowling tomorrow night with Marie and Stacy, and I was looking forward to it so much. I was going to borrow Dad's car, he'd already agreed, although Mom had to talk him into it. I was going to go out with the girls for the evening, and we were maybe going to meet some guys there. It was going to be a good wholesome, happy evening out. Nothing – I mean nothing – could possibly have gone wrong."

I take a deep breath, and then I turn to look first at Tom and then at Tanya.

"I just want my nice happy, normal life back," I add.

"Wow," Tanya says after a moment. "You know what? You're not bad at playing Jill. Not great, not as good as me, but... not bad."

"I'm not *playing* anyone," I tell her. "I'm Jill Cooper."

The door shudders again.

"We can't stay here," Tom says, as he starts limping toward the top of the steps that lead down toward the sound stage. "Those things will get through eventually, and I've got a feeling they won't be very happy."

"Wait," I reply, "we can't -"

"Do you have any better ideas?" he hisses, and he keeps going as he starts limping down the steps.

"My shrink is never going to believe this when I tell him," Tanya says as she walks over to join me. "I might need you guys to sign a statement, swearing you saw it all too." She sighs. "I'm actually starting to think that I'd have been better off if I'd stayed at the rehab facility."

"Why *did* you come here tonight?" I ask her.

She opens her mouth to reply, and then she hesitates for a moment.

"To fetch something," she says, and then she sets off after Tom.

"Wait!" I call after her, but then I remember that I have to keep my voice down.

I look at the backs of the nearby figures, and

I once again see the charred, veined insides of their hollow-out heads. A shudder passes through my chest, and after a few seconds I realize that I can't possibly stay up here with these things, so I start making my way carefully down the steps.

Ahead, I can see the kitchen and front room out my family's home. From here, they look like the sets in some cheap TV show, but I know that's not what they are. I live in that house, at 544 Horsemeadow Lane, with my family and nothing can make me believe anything different. All I need to do is get rid of Tom and Tanya somehow, and then I can go back to my bedroom and get to sleep. When I wake up in the morning, everything will be back to normal and I'll realize that this whole experience has just been a nightmare. And the best thing about nightmares is that you soon forget them, and they just fade away to nothing.

Once I reach the bottom of the steps, I see that Tom is already in the kitchen, while Tanya is a little way behind.

Turning, I look back up at the rows of seats. They look empty now, but I know that those figures are still out there. I don't understand how they're invisible from the front but visible from the back, but then again there's a lot about tonight that I don't understand.

"This is totally surreal," Tom says as I hurry past the snaking cables that run between the cameras, and finally catch up to him and Tanya. Looking around, he seems to be genuinely in awe. "I watched this show. I mean, it was always kind of lame, but I still ended up watching it with my family. Now I'm here, and it all looks so..."

He pauses.

"Cheap," he adds.

"Excuse me?" Tanya and I both reply, at the exact same time.

"Look at it," he continues, pressing a hand against the kitchen counter, causing it to creak slightly. "It's so flimsy. I guess that must be why *Litchford Life* is still the only major show that doesn't shoot in HD. It'd cost a fortune to rebuild the entire set."

"Alright, Mr. Critical," Tanya says, clearly annoyed, "do you wanna poke holes in anything else while you're trespassing here? 'Cause it doesn't make you smart, you know. It just makes you a negative idiot."

Stepping over to the kitchen table, I realize that I'm starting to feel light-headed. I take a deep breath and tell myself that everything's getting back to normal now, but then I turn and see that the rows of seats are still visible. It's weird, I know that there's usually a fourth wall over there, but I just can't quite remember what it looks like. I wait, convinced that reality will return at any moment, yet that missing wall stays missing.

"Some of this stuff's real," Tom says as he limps over to the other counter. "You've got a real kettle, a real microwave. A real fridge."

"We actually use some of that stuff during breaks," Tanya explains. "People think everything in Hollywood's luxurious, but it's not quite like that. I know how to heat up noodles in that microwave."

"Your poor thing," I reply.

She turns to me.

"I love noodles that have been done in the microwave," I tell her. "They're, like, my favorite thing ever."

"Are you in deep immersion for the role?" she asks. "I swear, you're creepily like Jill Cooper. You're not perfect, you're not as good as me, but you're not awful."

"Shut up," I mutter. "I just -"

"Don't you dare tell me to shut up!" she yells suddenly, storming over to me and shoving me back against the wall, which wobbles alarmingly. "I'm a goddamn star and you're nothing!"

"Shut up!" Tom snaps from behind her, and he clamps a hand over her mouth. She struggles, but he's holding her tight. "We can't risk you waking those creatures up in the seats. If you don't learn to keep your voice down, we'll have to gag you. Now, I need you to think real hard. From here, what's the easiest route out of this place?"

Before Tanya can say anything, however, we

all hear a creaking sound coming from somewhere beyond the kitchen, and we turn to look at the door that leads into the front room.

"Who else is here?" Tom whispers. "Could it be more of those things? Could they have found a way through the back?"

I open my mouth to answer, but at that moment I realize I can hear footsteps and voices.

Familiar voices.

"Mom," I whisper, as I spot shadows moving in the front room. "Dad..."

A second later, Dad steps bleary-eyed into view. He's tying the front of his dressing gown and rubbing his eyes, and Mom follows with her hair in a net and her white night mask smeared all over her face, with just two spaces where she'd usually have cucumber slices on her eyes.

"What's going on in here?" Dad asks, before stopping as soon as he sees the three of us. "What the..."

"I can explain!" I say, hurrying over to him. I've never been so pleased to see anyone in all my life. "You won't believe this, Dad, but I've had the craziest night in the history of the world. I swear, I only came down to get a glass of water. I don't even do that usually, but something just seems different about all of tonight and I came down, and then everything just seemed wrong."

"You're not making any sense, sweetheart,"

Mom says, coming closer to me and putting a hand on my forehead. "You don't have a fever, do you?"

"I wish I did," I tell her. "I wish that was the explanation, but..."

My voice trails off, and then I look out at the rows of seats again.

"What do you see," I ask, pointing at the seats, "over there?"

"What are you talking about?" Dad replies.

"Humor me," I continue, and now I can feel my chest tightening with anticipation. "It's important, Dad. Mom, you too. Just tell me what you see over at that end of the kitchen."

"Jill -"

"Just tell me!" I shout, before remembering that I mustn't make too much noise. Turning, I look out at the seats, but there's no hint of movement.

"I see the mirror on the wall," Dad tells me, looking the same way, "and I see..."

His voice trails off. I wait for him to continue, but he seems pretty spooked by something and after a moment he takes a couple of steps toward the missing wall. I desperately want him to tell me that everything's alright and that he just sees an ordinary wall, but as the seconds tick past I'm starting to realize that he can tell something's wrong.

"Dad?" I say cautiously.

"Phil?" Mom adds, making her way over to

join him. "Phil, honey, what's wrong?"

"I don't see the wall," he replies, his voice filled with a sense of wonder.

"What do you mean?" she asks. "It's right there."

"No, it's not," he continues. "I mean, it is, but it isn't at the same time. It's fading, and I can see... I can see empty seats."

I take a deep breath as a shudder passes through my chest. If Dad sees the same thing that I see, then that really ends any hope I had that this might all be in my head. Still, Dad will know what to do. Dad always saves the day, and I have no doubt whatsoever that he's going to know exactly what's happening and how we're going to deal with it.

I wait, but he says nothing.

"I think I see it too," Mom whispers. "There's something else out there. It's dark, it's like a huge empty mouth with teeth and... No, not teeth. Seats. There are lots of seats." She turns to Dad. "Phil, why are there seats over there?" she asks, her voice suddenly filled with panic. "Phil, what's going on?"

"Patrick?" Tanya says, heading over to Mom and Dad, and then nudging Dad's arm. "Come on, Patrick, what are you doing here so late at night? You're always the one who insists we get taping over with by nine. Why are you and Alison still here, and why are you still in character?"

"Who are you?" Dad asks, turning first to her and then to me. "Jill, who's this doppelganger. Where did you find her?"

"This has to be some kind of reality TV crap," Tanya says with a sigh. "Okay, so Herman getting killed was a special effect. It was a good special effect, but it still wasn't real. It was just some kind of next-grade bullshit. Wait, is this a crossover episode? Are we doing something that's half *Litchford Life* and half *The Twilight Zone*? Because I'm totally down with that, but I really think you should have warned me first!"

"Something's out there," Mom says, making her way toward the fourth wall, toward the cameras and the first row of seats beyond. "I can hear something moving."

"Don't go too far!" I call out to her, before setting off after her. "Mom, I'm serious, we don't know what those things are, but they're definitely dangerous!"

"I can hear some of the seats creaking," she continues, stepping over the snaking wires and cables that connect the various cameras. "Phil, I don't understand, it's as if our house is part of some kind of set. It's as if everything's suddenly not real." She holds her hands up. "I should have hit the wall by now. Even if I hadn't, I should be in the neighbors' garden. That stupid dog should be barking at me, but instead I'm..."

"Mom, get back!" I hiss as she gets closer to the first set of seats.

Hearing a clattering sound, I turn and see that Tanya has climbed onto one of the sideboards and is attempting to reach the top of a cupboard.

"What are you doing?" I ask her.

"What I came here for," she replies through gritted teeth. "Whatever you idiots are up to, I'm getting my photos back and then I'm out of here."

"What photos?"

"Don't be naive," she says with a sigh, struggling to reach the top section. "We've hidden all sorts of crap all around this set. There are Nazi swastikas, dirty photos and all sorts of other things just out of sight. People tune in thinking they're getting a good wholesome show, and they have no idea that there's all this filth just out of sight." She reaches up higher, and now she's really straining. "The thing is," she adds, "my contribution was a few photos that I really don't think should be in the public domain. They were even very slightly in a shot in one episode, but of course nobody could make them out. Damn it, can someone please help me here?"

Before I can reply, I hear Mom scream, and I turn to see that she's on her knees in front of the empty seats. I hurry forward, but Tom and Dad both grab me and hold me back as Mom turns and staggers back toward us. She's clutching her right arm, which is bleeding heavily.

"Something bit me!" she sobs as she puts her arms around Dad. "I didn't see what it was, but something actually bit me!"

"Let me see," he replies, briefly examining her wound before pulling her back toward the door. "This isn't right. This isn't happening."

"What do we do?" Mom sobs.

"I'll tell you exactly what we're going to do," he says. "We're going to go back to bed."

"Are you serious?" I stammer.

"Everyone's going back to bed!" he shouts angrily, and it's clear that he's getting really agitated now. "I mean it! In the morning everything will be fine, but first we have to go back to bed."

"But -"

"And that's an order!" he yells at me. "Don't defy me, Jill! You should never have gotten out of bed in the first place, this is all your fault, do you hear me? You are *so* grounded!"

"Where the hell are those photos?" Tanya mutters, still searching the tops of the cupboards. "Please, for the love of all that's holy, tell me someone didn't find them and sell them to one of the tabloids. I would never be able to live that down."

"Dad," I say, heading over to him as I feel tears welling in my eyes, "I don't think you understand what's happening here. There's an actual -"

"I see the wall again!" he snaps.

"What?"

"Over there!" he shouts, pointing past me. "It's back! It was never really gone in the first place, Jill. You just got into my head, that's all. I don't know what's wrong with you, but we're going to have a serious talk in the morning and I hope you don't think you're still going bowling with your friends, because you're grounded for a week!"

"Dad -"

"Two weeks!"

"Dad, please, be -"

"A month!" he roars, and then he turns and leads Mom back through to the hallway and over to the bottom of the stairs as she starts sobbing wildly. "You'll be lucky if you ever see the outside world again, Jill Cooper! I can't believe you've terrified your mother like this! You'll be doing all the chores around this house for the next year!"

I hurry through to the hallway, but they're already halfway up the stairs.

"What's happening?" my brother Mickey calls out from his room. "Why is everyone shouting?"

"No-one's shouting!" Dad yells at him. "Go back to bed!"

"Philip?" Grandma says from her room.

"What -"

"Go to bed!" he yells. "Jill's just playing a prank, that's all! We're not falling for it. There's going to be one hell of a family meeting in the morning!"

I open my mouth to call after them all, but then I hear their doors slamming shut and I realize that they're all just going to go to bed and pretend like nothing's wrong. I can't believe my family could be that crazy, and I tell myself that my best bet is to go up there and haul them all back downstairs, but a moment later I hear a gasping sound and I turn to see that Tom is struggling to limp over to me.

"They're coming!" he gasps.

"We really have to get out of here," I say as I hurry over and support him. Looking across at the counter, I see that Tanya is *still* searching for some dumb bunch of pictures. "Hey!" I yell. "Would you mind telling us the quickest way out of here?"

"Just a moment," she says, as she checks the top of the last cupboard. "I can't let those photos get out, they'd totally ruin my career." She turns to me. "There are pictures of me and a few guest actors doing something on the set of this show that we really shouldn't have been doing, if you catch my drift. Pictures of me snorting certain substances up my nose. If the press got hold of those, my dumbass family and manager would totally be given control over my entire life and I'd never be free again."

"We're going to die!" I tell her, as I look back across the kitchen and realize that I can hear the sound of footsteps approaching. "Don't you get it? The rest of them are awake and they're coming for us! We have to leave right now!"

"Relax," she replies, "they seem pretty slow. As soon as I've found the photos, I'll lead us to one of the side exits. We'll be out of here in ninety seconds maximum, but not until I've got the photos. So why don't you help me look?"

"Where are they?" I ask, trying not to panic.

"One or two of the others had a dumb game," she explains. "We'd try to hide really shocking things so that a few of the main stars would see them during a taping. It was our way of getting them to screw up their lines. Yes, I know it sounds really immature right now, but it was fun at the time." She sighs. "So, really, those photos could be more or less anywhere on the set."

"The creatures -"

"They hate water!" she snaps.

"What?"

"Didn't you notice, back in the office?" she continues. "I threw the vodka at them and they recoiled like a bunch of bitches. So obviously they hate water, or liquid, or something like that. Just splash them to keep them away."

"Are you insane?" I ask. "That's just about

the dumbest idea I've ever heard in my life."

"Oh yeah?"

Climbing down from the counter, she heads to the fridge and pulls it open. Taking out a bottle of mineral water, she unscrews the cap and then splashes the water across the room. Sure enough, some of the water hits something invisible and we all hear a cry of pain.

"Proof of concept," Tanya says, throwing the bottle to me. "Now, do you mind helping out? Keep those things back until I can get those photos." She climbs back onto the counter. "I will *not* have some production manager or set decorator make millions by selling me out to one of those disgusting websites."

I look across the room, and I swear I can hear footsteps coming this way. Figuring that I need to do something, I try splashing some water into thin air, and a moment later one of the creatures briefly becomes visible. It turns and pulls away, but already I can hear more footsteps heading toward us.

"There's no more in here!" I shout as I check the fridge, and then I hurry to the sink and try to refill the bottle, only to find once again that the faucet is fake. "Exactly where do you suggest I should get some water *from*?"

"I don't know," Tanya replies, "but so far you're doing a really lousy job of keeping us all safe, did you realize that? Improvise!"

"How?" I yell. "This is totally ridiculous! Just tell us which way to go, and we'll leave! I refuse to die here just be cause you lost a few stupid photos!"

"Sprinklers," Tom gasps.

Turning, I see that he's slumped in one of the chairs, and that he seems to be barely conscious.

"Sprinklers," he continues, and he manages to look up and point toward the gantry high above us. "You need to set the sprinklers off."

"How do I do that?" I ask.

He tries to say something, but his head slumps forward and I quickly realize that he's lost consciousness.

"How do I make the sprinklers work?" I yell, crouching next to him and shaking his shoulder. "I don't know what to do!"

"Fire," he whispers, as he briefly stirs a little.

"How do I start a fire?" I shout, but this time he's properly out.

Getting to my feet, I look all around. Footsteps are slowly coming closer and closer, but I don't see any way I can set a fire going. I rush over to the oven and try to turn it on, but – as I expected – it's just a dummy.

"Tanya," I say, turning to her, "I really think -"

Suddenly she slips and falls from the counter. I watch in horror as she lands awkwardly, and her right ankle breaks and twists in an awkward direction as she screams and slumps to the floor.

"Are you okay?" I yell, rushing over and dropping to my knees.

"Do I look like I'm okay?" she shouts, before letting out a primal cry of pain. "Damn, I hate my life!"

"Is there anything here I can use to start a fire?" I ask. "Do you have a cigarette lighter or anything like that?"

"Don't be gross," she replies, scrunching her nose up. "Why would I risk premature aging when I have skin that's *this* good? You have no idea how -"

"Can you walk on that ankle?"

"I'm not leaving without those photos!"

"Would you rather get eaten alive by those creatures?" I shout, as I look back across the room and see that one of the chairs is getting nudged aside. "They're moving slowly, but they're coming for us," I continue. "Are those photos worth your life?"

"I'd rather die than let those get out!"

I hesitate for a moment, and then I happen to spot the microwave again. Glancing back at the table, I see that there's a tablecloth, and in that moment I come up with an idea.

"We need fire," I stammer, getting to my

feet. "I'm going to make fire."

"How?" Tanya asks as I grab the tablecloth and pull it away, before rushing over and shoving it into the microwave. "It won't burn enough!"

"That's not the plan," I say as I start pulling the drawers open, desperately searching for cutlery. "You said the microwave's real, didn't you?"

"It's just about the only thing in this damn place that is," she replies.

"Then I just need some metal." Pulling open another drawer, I finally find all the knives and forks. When I grab some, however, I find that they're all made of plastic. "Where are the real ones?"

"The network wouldn't let us have any," Tanya replies, wincing with pain as she tries and fails to get to her feet. "Something about dangerous items in the workplace."

"You've got to be kidding me," I say as I realize that I don't see any other metal anywhere around. "There has to be something we can use."

Completely at a loss, I blank for a moment, but then I hear Tanya letting out another gasp of pain. Turning to her, I see something glinting on her face, and that's when I realize that her nose ring might just save day.

"Give me your ring!" I yell, rushing back over to her.

"What?"

"The ring in your nose! Give it to me!"

"Absolutely not!" she spits back at me. "Are you -"

"Give it to me!"

Unable to wait a moment longer, I grab her face and start trying to slide the ring out. She immediately starts fighting back, but I know that I don't have time for a proper fight so I pull on the ring instead, determined to rip it out.

Tanya screams and tries to punch me, but I duck out of the way while still pulling on the ring. The damn thing is stuck pretty tight, but I'm determined to pull it out of Tanya's septum so I press my feet against the lower cupboards and pull as hard as I can.

Howling in pain, Tanya tries to swat me away. I can feel the ring starting to come loose, but I still can't quite rip it away. I lunge at Tanya and slam her against the cupboard, and then I twist the ring again and try to pull it from a different angle. She squeals and tries again to hit me, but at that moment I feel a tearing sensation and I see blood gushing onto my hands.

"I'm sorry," I grunt, "but this is the only -"

And then, suddenly, I hear laughter.

Lots of laughter.

I pull for a moment longer, and then I freeze as I turn and look back across the kitchen. Laughter is ringing out all across the room, and the sound is coming from the direction of the missing fourth wall. I can hear lots and lots of different voices chuckling and guffawing, and after a few seconds I begin to realize that I've heard this exact same type of laughter before. It's been ever-present throughout my life, as if it's somehow been in the background of everything that's happened in this house, except now it's getting much louder. In some strange way, I can tell that these invisible figures are laughing at *me*, and my stunned expression seems only to be making them more amused.

"What the hell is that?" Tanya asks. "It sounds like the laugh track they pipe in during taping."

"You don't have an actual audience?" I reply.

"Sure, but they don't ever laugh enough, so we top it up with..."

I turn to her, and at that moment the laughter becomes much louder and stronger.

"They're dead people," she continues.

"What?"

"The laughter track we use is one that a lot of shows use," she explains, her voice filled with fear. "I've always thought it's kind of freaky. They were mostly recorded back in, like, the fifties and sixties. If you think about it, it stands to reason that most of the people who laughed on those recordings are dead now. Believe me, during taping sessions I used to hate it when the track was really turned up to maximum volume." She slowly looks back over across the kitchen. "Those voices... the laughter you're hearing now... it's dead people."

The laughter slowly starts dying down, and a moment later something invisible bumps the table. I quickly realize that the figures are coming again, so I turn back to Tanya.

"Wait," she says, looking down at her own bleeding nose, "please -"

Before I even have time to think, I yank the ring as hard as I can, finally tearing it out of her septum. She cries out and falls forward, and she puts her hands over her nose as blood gushes from the wound.

Looking down into my hands, I see the bloodied nose ring. I rush over to the microwave and shove the ring in along with the tablecloth, and then I slam the door shut before turning the setting up to maximum and hitting the button to the start the cooking process. Stepping back, I watch as the ring starts to turn on the plate, but so far nothing seems to be happening.

"You bitch!" Tanya screams, trying to get up but then letting out a yelp of pain as soon as she puts any pressure on her damaged ankle. "That ring is worth over a thousand dollars!"

"It's worth a lot more than that if it -"

Suddenly I see flames and sparks in the

microwave, accompanied by a loud popping sound, and that's my cue. Rushing forward, I open the door and pull the burning tablecloth out. I set it on the table, and already smoke is rising high up toward the gantry. Stepping back, I feel my heart racing as I hear more footsteps coming around either side of the table, and then I grab Tom's chair and pull it back so that he's closer to us. He's still unconscious, but when I nudge his shoulder he begins to stir slightly.

"I'm going to sue you when this is over" Tanya yells at me. "Do you hear me? I'm going to sue you into oblivion! That ring was -"

Before she can finish, the sprinklers activate, dousing the entire space with water. Alarms start ringing all around us, and at the same time I hear moans coming from the invisible figures as they start to retreat.

And then, as quickly as they activated, the sprinklers shudder to a halt.

"What happened?" I ask, as the tablecloth continues to burn and the alarms still ring out. "Why did they stop?"

"Do you seriously think a place like this is properly maintained?" Tanya hisses. "The insurance company's been onto the studio for years to fix all that crap, but did they ever listen? Hell, no!"

I watch in horror as a section of the burning tablecloth falls onto the floor, and the plastic covering immediately starts to burn.

"We have to get out of here," I say, as I start to lift a slurring, mumbling Tom up from the chair. "You said there's another exit, right? We have to find it!"

"This way," she replies, hauling herself up and leaning against the counter.

Supporting Tom on one side, I grab hold of Tanya and somehow the three of us manage to start stumbling through into the front room. When we reach the door that leads through into the laundry room, I stop and look back, and I see that the flames have really taken hold now. The entire kitchen is on fire, and in an instant I realize that I have to wake everyone else up before the house burns down.

"Wait here!" I shout, as I set Tom down on a chair and race to the stairs.

"Where the hell are you going?" Tanya yells.

"I have to get Mom and Dad and the others!"

"There's nothing up there, you moron!"

Ignoring her, I run up the stairs, and then at the last moment I manage to stop myself as I find that the upper level of the house has completely disappeared. I almost topple over the edge, and then I look down and see that somehow all the bedrooms are down on the ground floor, arranged next to the kitchen and the front room. I can see other familiar places, too, including the garden and – somehow – Dad's office at work.

Turning, I look the other way, and instead of seeing the street I find myself looking down at my friend Stacy's bedroom. It's as if every place that I regularly visit is somehow here, laid out around our house in some kind of studio setting, and after a few seconds I take a step back as I start feeling light-headed. My whole world is set out below me, and for the first time I'm starting to realize that it's so cheap and poorly-built. Even as smoke rises from the kitchen, I can't quite believe that this is really happening, and then I look up and see that I'm pretty close to the lighting gantry and the useless sprinklers.

None of this is real. I feel... weightless.

"Hurry!" Tanya screams from down below. "We have to get out! Now!"

Forcing myself to stay focused, I scramble back down the stairs. Tanya's trying to hold Tom up, but her ankle is too badly damaged, so I help them both and we make our way through into the laundry room, which somehow now leads to the back of the studio. We head through a set of double doors, and we emerge in yet another corridor.

"There's a fire exit along here," Tanya says, as the three of us struggle toward another door. "I used to sneak out for a break whenever filming got too much. Hopefully it's still unlocked."

Sure enough, when we reach the door, it opens easily. I help Tom through, and then I freeze as I feel a cold breeze against my face. Looking outside, I see that we're in some kind of dark alley behind a large building, and I hear the sound of cars in a nearby street. I've been outside at night before, of course, but somehow this is completely new. The sights and sounds and smells are astonishing, and for a few seconds I'm lost for words as I look up at the sky and see nothing but darkness.

This world feels so much more real, so much more alive and vibrant.

"Move!" Tanya says, shoving us forward.

Turning, I see that she's stepping back into the burning building, as sirens ring out in the distance.

"Where are you going?" I ask.

"I just remembered where those goddamn photos are going to be," she replies. "Don't worry, I'll be two minutes at most, I need to get to the dressing room. I guarantee the photos are hidden behind the filing cabinet. I remember now, one of the other actors had a bit of a stash there."

"You can't go back inside," I tell her, but I'm too late and she's already rushing back along the corridor.

The door swings shut, and now the sirens are getting closer. I let Tom down onto a nearby crate so that he can rest, and then I glance along the alley and see the most amazing bright lights ahead. It's as if the world has exploded in my eyes and become so much more real, and I can't help but slip away from Tom and start making my way toward the lights. The world seems to be luring me onward, and finally I reach the end of the alley and I let out a stunned gasp as I see and hear the roaring, rushing tumult of a city that's so much larger than anything I ever imagined in all my life.

"It's on fire!" a voice yells nearby, and people are rushing toward the theater, but I barely notice them as I start to move across the sidewalk.

Everything's so huge and tall out here, and I'm having to fight a strong sense of nausea as I step off the sidewalk and -

Suddenly a huge bus rushes past me, almost hitting me. I feel the air swirling as I edge back onto the sidewalk, and a moment later a passerby bumps against me.

"Watch where you're going," he says, but he's gone before I can utter an apology.

As fire trucks pull up nearby, I look around at the huge buildings and I feel utterly dwarfed by the scale of this city. From various signs all around, I can tell that I must be in New York, and I swear the immense rushing onslaught of the place is making me feel weak. Part of me wants to run and hide, but part of me wants to keep my eyes open and take in every moment of this absolute insanity.

In the end, all I can do is continue to turn and look at all the brightness, and listen to all the roars, and breathe in the incredible smells of a world that I'm seeing for the first time. I swear, I feel as if I'm actually living for the first time ever.

****

"Hey, are you okay in here?"

Turning, I see that Tom is standing in the doorway, and I realize that it's been a few minutes since I came through to the kitchen to fetch some snacks. I stare at my husband for a moment, at his rugged good looks that somehow are only enhanced by his scars, and then I smile.

"I'm fine," I tell him. "Tell Monica and Ashley that I'll be right through."

He heads back into the front room, and I take a deep breath. It's been ten years now since I left the studio in New York, and I still have moments when I feel as if I'm not quite used to the sheer intensity of the real world. Here in our house in Beverly Hills, we have every luxury and every convenience, thanks to the life I slipped into. After all, I look and sound exactly like Tanya Simmonds, and after she failed to make it out of the burning studio everyone just assumed that I was her. I was forced into some rehab facility, but I quickly proved that I was free of any drug or alcohol problems, and

I was released. I had no interest in acting or singing, so I invested Tanya's fortune and made a whole load more money from the business world.

And I married Tom. None of this would be possible without him.

There are times when I still feel as if I belong back in that other world, as if I'm a fish out of water, but I've managed to cut those times down to brief flashes. The real world is so much more complicated, and I've had to rapidly get up to speed with all the politics and stuff that I never noticed before; now I know who Donald Trump and Barack Obama and Ronald Reagan and all these people are, people who never featured in my old life. The most surprising thing, however, is the sheer level of detail in the real world. Even now, as I reach down and touch the counter-top, I can't help but think back to the kitchen at 544 Horsemeadow Lane, where everything was simply designed to look decent on a TV broadcast. There were so many rough edges, and we never really noticed during our lives there, but now the difference is staggering.

"Honey!" Tom calls out. "It's on!"

"Coming."

Grabbing the snacks, I head out to the front room, where Tom and the kids are already in place on the sofa, getting ready for tonight's big event.

"Are you sure you want to watch this?" he asks cautiously. "If you'd rather not, we can -"

"Are you kidding?" I reply as I take a seat next to him. "I wouldn't miss it for the world. The final ever episode of *Litchford Life* is a huge event. It's been on for almost twenty seasons."

"And you don't regret turning down the chance to appear in the last episode?"

"Not one bit," I reply, as I look toward the screen and wait for this batch of commercials to end.

The truth is, going back to the set was never an option. After the fire, the entire thing was rebuilt from scratch and the show continued, although I – or rather, Tanya Simmonds – never returned. Some people speculated that the show would fail without Jill Cooper, but if anything it soared, especially after my nerdy cousin was added to the line-up on a permanent basis. I've avoided watching whole episodes, mainly because it's too sad to see Mom and Dad and the others, but I've caught glimpses and tonight I want to see the show out. I want closure.

Besides, people are missing the point when they claim that Jill isn't on *Litchford Life*.

She's still there, if you know where to look.

A few viewers began to point her out online after the show returned from its fire-induced break. In several episodes, about two or three a year, Jill is faintly visible in the back of a few shots, lurking in the shadows. She's not dressed like Jill, she's dressed like Tanya, but she's just about visible once you know where to look. The producers have vehemently denied that they're responsible, although most people figure that this is just some kind of weird trick. One or two particularly conspiratorial viewers have suggested that somehow Jill's ghost is appearing on the show, although they've never really been able to explain how or why that would happen, especially since Jill was simply written off in a few lines that explained she'd gone to live on the other side of the country. Plus, everyone knows that Tanya Simmonds is still alive, right?

Right?

Except she never made it out of that building. I don't know why a body wasn't found, but it's not my job to explain every part of what happened. I can't explain much of it at all, to be honest.

So now we settle down to watch the historic, one hour final episode of *Litchford Life*, and about halfway through I spot Jill in the back of a scene, staring at the camera. Or, rather, I spot Tanya Simmonds. She's only there for a few seconds, but that's enough for me to wonder what will happen to her once the sets have been torn down and the studio space has been allocated to some other production. Will she just haunt that place forever, or will the end of the show allow her some peace?

Well, again...

Not my problem.

The show's pretty funny, though. Tom and I laugh, and so do the children. So do the members of the audience and the voices captured on those old recordings from half a decade ago. The voices of the dead.

***

Opening my eyes, I find myself staring up at the darkness of the bedroom ceiling. I blink a couple of times, and then I glance at the bedside clock and see that it's almost 3am. I wake up at 3am almost every single night, and although I usually manage to get back to sleep, I often have a few minutes of quiet contemplation.

Not tonight, however.

Tonight, I sit up and listen to the silence of the house. Tom is gently snoring next to me, and when I head onto the landing and look into the kids' room I see that they're asleep too. It's somehow very calming to see that my family is resting and safe, and as I head downstairs to fetch a glass of water I can't help but reflect upon the fact that I'm so very blessed.

Once I'm in the kitchen, I pour myself some water and I start to drink as I look out the window. Los Angeles is laid out before me, sparkling in the darkness. The real world is so much busier and more vibrant than the life I lived in that studio, and I'm so thankful that I live *here* now, despite all the loudness and drama that seems to be filling our lives. Politics, crime, celebrity, sport... I find the real world to be so much richer, but also so hard to keep track of. It's exhilarating, that's what it is, and I love it more than ever.

After setting my glass down, I turn to go back upstairs, but then I freeze. Looking toward the far end of the kitchen, I realize that I can't see the fourth wall. I swallow hard, waiting for my vision to clear, and then I take a couple of steps forward. I know there's a wall there, but I still don't see it, not even after I make my way all the way around the dining table.

Stopping, I stare into the void. For a moment, I consider going out there further to prove to myself that the missing wall is real, but I manage to stop myself. I take a deep breath, and then I turn and head to the stairs. And as I head up to the bedroom, to slide back into my spot next to my husband, I refuse to let myself look back. This time, I'm going to play it safe. In the morning, that wall will be right back in place, and I'll be able to forget all about the void that I saw, and the darkness, and even the strange cable that I spotted snaking its way across the floor.

THE COUGH

As soon as the car pulled up in the driveway, Kerry scrambled out, almost stumbling in the process. She raced around to the back and lifted the boot open, and then she scooped up all the bags and began to carry them to the house. Again, she almost tripped a few times, such was her haste to get inside; finally, however, she made it up onto the porch, where she realized she'd have to put the bags back down while she found her key.

"Damn it," she muttered under her breath, as she set the bags on the ground and started going through her pockets. "Come on, where are you?"

Glancing over her shoulder, she was at least relieved to not see anybody else in the area. Green rolling hills extended as far as the eye could see, and even the road was empty. A moment later, finally locating the key at the bottom of the wrong pocket, she turned and fumbled to get the door open.

***

"The important thing, I want to stress again," the man on the news said, "is that there's no need to panic. A lot of the strategies and safeguards that we developed during the Covid-19 pandemic will serve us well in this latest situation."

"Even though CERS-22 is estimated to be up to fifteen times as deadly as Covid-19 was?" the reporter asked.

"That number hasn't been confirmed," the man replied. "It's not helpful to spread numbers like that around. What we need right now is for everyone to stay calm and follow the rules until we know a little more about this new virus."

"That's easy for you to say," Kerry said, sitting on the edge of the chair with her arms around her knees, staring at the screen with a rapt, terrified expression on her face. "Stay calm and die, is that what we're supposed to do?"

She'd been waiting eagerly for the latest news broadcast to begin, but now Kerry found her attention wandering. She started looking around the gloomy, dusty front room of the cottage, and she was coming to realize that she'd have to do a little work to make the place truly safe. During the

Covid-19 pandemic a few years earlier, she'd stayed in London and hunkered down, and she'd made it through unscathed. Now that this new CERS-22 virus was breaking out, however, she'd decided that enough was enough, and she'd bolted for the old cottage that had been in the family for years, but which – for probate-related matters – had never been sold.

"And do masks help to reduce transmission of CERS-22?" the reporter asked, as Kerry turned back to look at the TV. "Again, there's been some very conflicting advice."

"I think it's safe to say that masks can't hurt," the man said cautiously. "Until we get some more information, there's no reason not to be -"

Suddenly her phone began to ring, and Kerry grabbed it from the dining room table. She saw her mother's face flashing up on the screen, and she quickly answered.

"I'm here," she said, and she realized she could see her own breath in the cold air. She made a mental note to get the boiler up and running. "I made it."

"That's good, darling," her mother replied. "Are you sure -"

"Are you and Dad on your way?"

"Well -"

"You're coming, aren't you?" she continued. "Tell me you haven't allowed Jacqui to talk you into staying."

"Your sister made some very good points," her mother said, sounding a little tired of the conversation already. "Your father and I are getting on, dear, and we'd just feel better staying at home. We can get our shopping delivered, and we managed perfectly well a few years ago during Covid."

"This is worse than Covid," Kerry pointed out. "Much worse."

"Well, that's what they say, but -"

"You can't stay in Medway!" Kerry snapped. "It's a breeding ground for this thing, it's way too close to London!"

"We've made our minds up," her mother replied. "We're staying put. We'll be fine, we've got Jacqui just around the corner and we learned a lot from last time this happened. Honestly, you mustn't worry about us too much."

"You're making a huge mistake," Kerry told her.

"Maybe. Oh, your father's calling me, I think he needs me in the kitchen. I'll call you back later, darling, okay?"

"Mum, listen, this is -"

Before she could finish, Kerry heard the click of the line being cut, and she realized her mother had put the phone down. She almost called her straight back, before stopping herself and leaning back in the chair. The voices on the TV were still arguing, but somehow she found herself unable to really focus on what they were saying. Instead, she was listening to the silence of the cottage, and she was coming to understand that she was truly isolated and alone. As far as she knew, there wasn't another soul within ten miles of the place. That fact was both comforting and disturbing, but she reminded herself that at least she was out of the cauldronous mix of London.

She took a deep breath, and then she switched the TV off and leaned back as she tried to calm her racing heart. She had enough supplies to last six months if necessary, and she was sure that things would calm down long before that time was up. She felt her heart rate slowing, and she took several more deep, slow breaths as she focused on the fact that her three hundred mile car journey was over. Now she could relax.

And then, from somewhere upstairs in the supposedly empty cottage, she heard a cough.

***

"Hello?" she asked a few minutes later, as – carrying a garden fork from outside for protection – she made her way cautiously up the stairs. "Is anyone there?"

The cough had been brief, and there had

only been one, but Kerry wasn't in the habit of doubting her own senses. She knew what she'd heard and, as she reached the halfway point of the staircase, she was already worrying that some drifter or hobo might have made a home in the cottage while it had been empty. She adjusted her grip on the fork's handle, even though she knew she'd never bring herself to actually use it against anyone, and a few seconds later she reached the top of the stairs, where one of the floorboards creaked beneath her right foot.

Looking around, she saw that the doors to the bathroom and the three bedrooms were all wide open.

"Hello?" she said again. "I'm armed, so you'd better not try anything. If anyone's here, you need to come out right now with your hands up. If you don't, I won't be held responsible for what happens next."

She waited, but the cottage remained stubbornly silent now, even though Kerry couldn't help imagining some murderous figure lurking in one of the rooms. She wanted to call the police, but she didn't much like the idea of anyone – even a police officer – entering the cottage and potentially bringing the virus; besides, she wasn't sure that she'd be taken too seriously if she started claiming that she'd heard a single random cough. Were there animals that made coughing sounds? Could the wind have been responsible? She was open to all possibilities, but she kept coming back to the fact that the cough had sounded an awful lot like a *human* cough.

Realizing that she couldn't just stand at the top of the stairs all afternoon, she finally edged closer to the nearest door, before rushing through with the fork raised.

Nothing.

Just a bed, and a dresser.

She leaned down to check under the bed, and then she headed back out onto the landing. She was feeling more and more certain that she'd imagined the whole thing, that some weird freak moment had caused the supposed cough, but she knew that she'd still have to check the cottage out. So she set about going from room to room, keeping the fork raised at all times, investigating every single spot where a person could conceivably hide. With every cupboard checked, every storage space opened, she felt a little more relieved, until finally she stood back out on the landing and realized that there was nowhere left for anyone to hide. She'd even checked the attic, braving the spiders and dirt, and found nothing.

The cough, then, must simply have been an aberration.

A fluke.

Feeling a lot calmer now, she made her way

back downstairs. She leaned the fork against the wall in the hallway, figuring that it might be wise to have some kind of weapon, and then she headed back through to the front room, where the TV was still running on silent.

And then, just as she was about to reach for the remote control, she heard the cough again.

***

"You heard *what*?" her mother asked over the phone.

"I'm not going crazy," Kerry replied, as she stood in the front room with her back to the wall, staring at the door that led into the hallway. She had the fork leaning on the armchair next to her. "It's happened three times now. I go up, I look around and make sure that no-one's up there, and then I come back down, and then I hear it again."

She waited for a response, but her mother said nothing.

"The first time," she continued, "I was just about able to convince myself that it was nothing. But this is three times now, Mum. Something or someone is coughing up there and I don't know what to do."

Again she waited, and again her mother didn't reply.

"I don't know what to do," she added.

"I was afraid something like this might happen," her mother muttered.

"What do you mean?"

Again, there was no immediate response.

"What do you mean, Mum?" she asked. "Why were you afraid something like this might happen?"

"Do you remember your Aunt Lucy?"

"Of course. Well, just about. I was too young to really know her, but I remember coming to visit her here a few times."

"There's a reason the cottage was left empty for so long while we tried to figure out the paperwork to sell it," her mother explained. "Your cousin Lou tried to live there for a while, but he..."

Her voice trailed off.

"What about him?" Kerry asked cautiously. "What happened?"

"You know Lou's a bit weird," her mother replied, "so at first we all thought that was what was going on. Lucy was sick in the last six months before she died, and she spent most of her time in bed. Lou claimed that once he moved in, after she'd died, he started to notice... odd things happening around the place."

"What kind of odd things?"

"Bumps. Little whispers." Her mother paused. "He also said he heard her coughing a few times."

"After she was dead?"

"Like I said, Lou's an odd one."

"Wait a minute," Kerry replied, "are you telling me that I've come to self-isolate in a haunted house?"

"Of course not! Ghosts don't exist. But Lou had a friend over to visit, and he claimed to hear the same things. They were probably egging each other on. Eventually Lou hired an exorcist, or a ghost-chaser, or whatever they're called, to try to rid the house of his mother's spirit. I feel ridiculous even saying all of this."

"This has to be a joke," Kerry said, her mind racing at the thought of such craziness.

"Eventually they managed to stop all the strange happenings," her mother continued. "I think they had to remove all of Lucy's belongings from the house, to kind of sever the link to her. That's what they claimed, anyway. They even got rid of her collection of porcelain cats. Do you remember how many she had? There were hundreds. Lou sold them all as a job lot to some weirdo from the internet, and after that he said the house was fine. Well, mostly."

"Mostly?"

"He left six months later, but he said the place was pretty much empty by then. He only heard one or two odd things during his final time there."

"One or two?" Kerry hesitated for a moment. "So Aunt Lucy's ghost *was* still here?"

"You can't take Lou too seriously. He's always been into that sort of thing. Don't you remember when he said he saw an alien on the train? He expected us all to believe that a real alien was just sitting on the train, reading a newspaper and commuting into the city. Kerry, I didn't mention any of this to you because I know it's a load of rubbish, and because I also know that you're in something of a heightened state. I didn't want to worry you."

Kerry kept her eyes fixed on the hallway.

"Kerry?" her mother continued. "Are you listening to me?"

"I am," she replied, before swallowing hard. "So the cottage is haunted and -"

"The cottage is not haunted!"

"I came here to get away from the world," Kerry continued, struggling to keep from panicking all over again. "I was so scared that I might catch CERS-22, I was constantly monitoring myself for the symptoms. You have no idea how many people were coughing in the street in London, it was a nightmare every time I left the house. So many people were coughing all the time, all around me, I felt like I was losing my mind. I came here because I wanted to be somewhere safe, and now you're seriously telling me that my dead aunt might still be here!"

"I can't talk to you when you're like this," her mother replied. "Kerry, you need to get a grip."

"Thanks, Mum," she said through gritted teeth. "Thanks a lot."

With that, she cut the call and tossed her phone onto the seat of the nearest armchair. Her head was spinning and she couldn't quite believe what she'd just heard, but at the same time she'd always believed that ghosts might exist. After all, how could humans possibly claim to understand everything about the world? She paused for a moment longer, and then she realized that if she wanted to have any chance of a peaceful stay at the cottage, she only had one option.

***

"Hey, Aunt Lucy, do you remember me?" she asked as she stopped in the doorway that led to the master bedroom. She was still holding the garden fork, just in case the ghost turned out to actually be a crazed homeless person. "It's little Kerry, I used to come here to visit you sometimes. You used to make biscuits for me, remember?"

She looked at the double bed, which she figured was where Lucy had spent her final months after she'd been diagnosed with...

What had she died off, again?

Kerry felt bad for not remembering, but she felt like it was something like pneumonia or an infection. Could pneumonia last six months? Now she wasn't sure, but she'd heard stories about Lucy being bedridden, coughing a lot and slowly getting thinner, and finally passing away. Kerry had only been about eight years old when that had happened, so her memory of the period was rather bare, but she knew that Lucy had lingered for a long time, and she figured it wasn't that surprising that the old woman had continued to linger after death.

Still, she wasn't keen on sharing the house with a ghost, so Kerry had already decided to finish the exorcism that had been started all those years ago.

"I'm just going to find what they missed," she said as she entered the room. "There's no need to be scared, Aunt Lucy. Obviously Lou and the others left something behind, something of yours that's still keeping you tethered to this place. Once I find that thing, you'll be free to finally leave. Doesn't that sound good?"

And don't I sound condescending? she thought as she looked around and tried to figure out where to start.

When Lou and his friend had emptied the house of Lucy's possessions, they'd clearly missed something, and Kerry assumed that the item in question must be fairly small. She made her way over to the wardrobe and pulled it open, and this time she took care to really lean in as far as she could manage in an effort to spot any last stray item. She had to bend over fully to see down into the murky bottom, but so far she could find nothing of Lucy's that night explain her continuing presence.

And then, suddenly, she heard another cough.

Standing bolt upright, Kerry immediately banged her head on the roof of the wardrobe. Letting out a gasp of pain, she spun around and looked back at the bed, and this time she felt certain that the cough had come from the exact spot where Lucy had spent her final months.

"Are you here?" she asked, her voice trembling with fear. "Aunt Lucy, if you can hear me, I'm doing this for your own sake. You don't want to be sitting around still, just haunting your old home, do you?"

She waited.

"*Do* you?"

She half expected a spectral vision of her aunt to appear on the bed, but nothing of the sort happened. Still, she couldn't shake the feeling that she was being watched, and that an invisible spectral version of her aunt might be sitting on the bed and scowling at her. She tried to put that image out of her mind, but finally she felt too uncomfortable and she hurried out of the room.

As soon as she was out on the landing, she heard another cough, coming from over her shoulder. Again, she spun around, and this time she hit the end of the garden fork on the side of the door, causing a loud clanging sound.

She stared at the bed, and now she felt certain that in some way her aunt was staring back at her.

"Stop looking at me like that!" she said firmly, still addressing the empty space on the bed. "Look, I know you're there, and I know it's you that keeps coughing. I don't know if you're doing it to deliberately annoy me, but it's going to stop and it's going to stop today, okay?"

She hesitated, expecting an answer.

"So cough all you like," she added finally, before turning to go and check another room. "I don't even care anymore!"

***

By the time night began to fall, Kerry still hadn't found anything that might be keeping Lucy linked to the house. She'd been through every room several times over, with no luck, and she was starting to get desperate.

She was also starting to get cold.

Having tried to turn the radiators on, she'd

found that something seemed to be stopping them. She'd tried fiddling with the boiler, but for some reason that seemed to be off, and she hadn't found time to take a closer look. She knew that at some point she was going to have to fiddle with the boiler and try to get it up and running, but she kept telling herself that first she was going to have to get rid of Lucy's ghost. Nothing mattered more than that.

Still carrying the garden fork, she traipsed back upstairs, letting the fork's prongs drag and bump against the steps. When she reached the top, she once again look through at the master bedroom.

"Can't you give me a clue?" she asked wearily. "All you do is cough. Is that what you want? Are you happy to spend eternity coughing in an empty house?"

She waited.

"Okay, cough now," she continued. "Right now, just to absolutely prove to me beyond a shadow of a doubt that you're really here. Can you do that?"

She waited.

She heard no cough.

"Or am I losing my mind?" she added, with a hint of tears in her eyes. "Is that what's going on? I've been here less than a day, and am I just not suited to being out here?"

She waited.

No cough.

"Fine," she muttered, turning and heading into the second bedroom, once again dragging the prongs of the garden fork along the floor, "*don't* help me. I mean, you could let me know what's keeping you here, so that I could find it and free you, but you have no obligation to do that."

She started once again checking the storage cupboard in the corner of the room, even though she'd checked it before. She was almost shivering now, but she told herself that she had no time to fix the boiler, not until she'd managed to rid the house of Aunt Lucy's ghost. There was no way she could actually sleep in the house if it was haunted, and she was already worried that she might have to sleep in her car. Or, worse, drive back to London.

"It's almost as if you enjoy this," she said under her breath, before stepping back and slamming the cupboard's door shut. "Is that it, Aunt Lucy? You know, I remember you being real nice when you were alive, but have you turned into some kind of asshole now that you're dead? Are you so bored that this is how you get your kicks?"

She waited a few seconds, giving time for a response, and then she stormed back out onto the landing.

"This whole haunting shtick is getting real old. Don't you have any imagination?"

She walked past the master bedroom, on her way to the bathroom, and yet again she dragged the fork.

"If I was as ghost," she continued, "I'd at least make an effort and -"

Before she could get another word out, she heard another cough coming from the master bedroom.

"That's it!" she yelled, turning to look back through to the double bed. "I'm not even -"

Suddenly she felt her left foot slip on the top step of the stairs. She reached out to steady herself, but in that moment she accidentally shifted her weight backward and she twisted around. She let out a faint cry as she fell down the stairs, and the last thing she thought was a simple hope.

Please don't land on the garden fork.

Please don't land on the garden fork.

Please don't land on the -

Slamming down into the floor down in the hallway, she immediately felt the fork's prongs driving into her torso, and then her head hit the boards and she was knocked out cold.

***

The first thing she noticed, as her eyes began to flicker open, was that she was absolutely freezing. The hallway was dark, which meant she'd been unconscious for at least a couple of hours, and a moment later she remembered the sensation of landing on the fork. There was no pain, at least not yet, but she was scared to look down in case she found that she was badly injured.

Finally, forcing herself to be brave, Kerry rolled onto her side and looked at the spot where the prongs had entered her body.

She paused, and then she reached down and carefully pulled the fork away. To her immense relief, she found that only one of the prongs had actually penetrated her skin, cutting into her body on one side of her waist, and it had only done so by a couple of centimeters. She figured she'd need a tetanus shot, but otherwise she seemed to have had an extremely lucky escape.

Sitting up, and pulled her shirt aside and examined the wound, which really didn't look too bad at all. She poked the damaged skin and immediately winced, and then she looked at the floorboards and saw that there was no massive pool of blood. In fact, the only blood was on her shirt, and on one prong of the fork.

"Thank God," she whispered, leaning back against the wall for a moment as she began to shiver in the freezing temperature. "That was close."

For a moment, she was unable to comprehend just how close she'd come to impaling herself. She looked up the stairs and thought back to that frantic moment when – driven half-crazy by the sound of another cough – she'd tripped and fallen.

The whole thing felt nuts now, although she couldn't help wondering whether the coughs had continued while she'd been knocked out. Reaching up, she checked her head for any blood, and then she hauled herself to her feet as she realized that she was going to have to do something about the heating.

Screw the fork, she figured; she'd been lucky not to freeze to death.

Limping through to the kitchen, and finding in the process that her right ankle was a little sore, she made her way over to the large wooden compartment on the far wall. She pulled the cover away, exposing the boiler, and then she reached inside so she could try to figure out what was wrong. As she did so, she heard another cough coming from somewhere in the house, but she only hesitated for a moment before getting back to work. Sure, she knew she had to get rid of the ghost still, but she also knew she had to save herself from an icy end. Her teeth was chattering, and she had no real idea how to work a boiler other than hitting the on-off switch, but she was desperately hoping for a miracle.

She hit the main switch a few times, but the boiler stubbornly refused to start working. That was pretty much the limit of her ability to get anything done. A moment later, just as she was about to go and fetch her phone in a last attempt to come up with a solution, she spotted something resting right at the back of the compartment.

She peered closer, and then she reached around and found, to her surprise, that a small porcelain cat was resting on its side. The cat was partially wedged against a black switch on the boiler's underside. Kerry hesitated, before sliding the cat out of the way.

Immediately, the switch was flicked and the boiler burst to life.

"Finally!" a voice said suddenly, and Kerry turned to see the ghostly figure of her Aunt Lucy standing right behind her. "That took you long enough, dear. Why didn't you just try to fix the boiler right at the start? At least you managed it eventually. That idiot son of mine never did. Now I can move on."

Suddenly she coughed.

"Oh," she added, rolling her eyes, "I hope that cough doesn't follow me to the next place. That'd be a pain in the -"

And then she was gone, in the blink of an eye, leaving Kerry standing frozen in place with the porcelain cat still in her right hand. She opened her mouth to say something, and then her knees buckled and she fainted.

***

The first thing she noticed, as her eyes began to

flicker open, was that she was nice and warm. The kitchen was dark, but as Kerry began to sit up she realized that the radiators were all running. She took a deep breath and saw that her breath was no longer visible, and then she noticed the porcelain cat resting nearby on the floor.

Scrambling to her feet, she grabbed the cat and limped to the back door. Once she was out on the freezing cold porch, she threw the cat as far as she could away from the property, and then she stepped back inside and slammed the door shut. Still not quite believing what had happened, she leaned against the door and tried to get her thoughts together, and then she heard a bumping sound coming from the hallway.

Startled, she looked through toward the bottom of the stairs, just as the radiator out there let out another bump. Sighing, Kerry realized that since the cottage's heating had been off for many years, she shouldn't be surprised if the system made a few noises during the night.

A noisy central heating system, she could handle.

Making her way through to the front room, she checked her phone and saw that she'd missed a few calls from her mother. She briefly considered not replying, but then she tapped to call her back anyway, figuring that she didn't want to call any worry.

"There you are," her mother said as soon as she answered. "And how are things going, dear? You're not still fretting about a few strange noises, are you?"

"I..."

Kerry paused as she heard the heating system let out another rumble, but she quickly reminded herself that there must simply be some air in the pipes. That, she knew, she could fix easily enough, so she focused on putting all the worries out of her mind.

"It's sorted," she said.

"But what about -"

"I told you, it's sorted," she added, interrupting her mother. She thought back to the sight of Aunt Lucy's ghostly figure, but she knew there was no point trying to explain all of that. Not right now, at least. "Mum, it's late," she added, "and I've had a really long day. You don't have to worry about me, okay?" She looked around the front room for a moment. "I actually think I'm going to like it here. I can work from home, and you know I've never had a problem being alone. It's not ideal, but I'll muddle through."

"Well, that's certainly an improvement from earlier," her mother replied. "Your father and I were getting a little worried, darling."

"Is Jacqui bringing you some food?"

"She's bringing moussaka tomorrow."

"That sounds really nice," she said, feeling a pang of regret that she wouldn't be with the rest of her family, but quickly reminding herself that she had no real reason to feel too sorry for herself. "Is it okay if I call you tomorrow? I need to sort a few things out here before I hit the sack. And Mum..."

She paused.

"I think Aunt Lucy's okay," she continued. "Wherever she is, I mean. I mean... I don't actually know what I'm trying to say. I guess I just don't want you to worry about her. I think she's fine."

"I certainly hope so," her mother replied. "Now, make sure you look after yourself in that place. I want you to try not to stress so much. You've always been such a worrywart, Kerry. This CERS-22 is horrible, of course, but try to make the best of it. Try to unwind."

"I will," Kerry said. "Speak to you tomorrow. Bye, Mum."

With that, she cut the call and went back to the kitchen. The boiler was still running healthily, so she took a moment to make herself a cup of tea, which she then carried into the front room. She plopped herself down onto the most comfortable armchair, and she took a deep breath as she realized that her first day at the cottage hadn't gone too badly. She'd freed the ghost of her aunt, and now she just had to get through six months of solitude. She had her laptop, she had plenty of work to get done, and she felt slightly guilty for looking forward to so much peace and quiet. The heating system let out another bump, but she didn't let that bother her at all. Finally, after so much craziness, Kerry allowed herself to relax.

And then, suddenly, she coughed.

THE HAUNTING OF WIND'S END COTTAGE

"He's coming!"

"Crap..."

After swiftly downing the rest of his pint, Malcolm Lugford scrambled from his bar stool and followed everyone else out the back door of *The Restful Sailor*.

Scarcely had that door swung shut, than the front door creaked open and the lumbering frame of Colin Obford stepped into view, silhouetted against the rainy weather that had for several hours now been dousing the tiny coastal town of Feldown.

"Evening, Colin," the landlord said with a weary sigh, as he began to collect the various empty glasses from the bar.

"And good evening to you, my fine friend," Colin replied, eyeing the glasses with curiosity before stepping fully into the bar area and letting the front door fall shut. "Am I to take it, by the sight of so many used receptacles, that I have once again arrived shortly after the departure of everybody else?"

"You have a knack for that, Colin," the landlord muttered bitterly, as he thought of all the custom that was regularly driven away in the evenings by Colin's arrival.

"That is most distressing," Colin replied, making his way over to the bar and taking a look at the ale selection. "You know, I even started dropping by a little earlier after my evening walk, in the hope that I might bump into a fellow drinker. Why, I don't think I've encountered anybody here since two weeks ago, when Jack Laggy was still in the booth over in the far corner."

"I remember," the landlord said, thinking back to that unfortunate night when Jack's trouser leg had caught on a nail, which had kept him firmly in place and had resulted in him having to 'enjoy' Colin's company for several hours.

"I suppose I shall try this one," Colin announced, tapping one of the pumps. "I trust that it has been kept correctly, and that I shall not be served a pint of warm sludge?"

"I do my best, Colin."

"You're the landlord of a public house," Colin pointed out with a chuckle. "If you can't keep your ale in the proper condition, then really what good are you at all? It's hardly rocket science."

"Indeed, Colin," the landlord replied as he began to pour the man a pint. "This one's from a brewery not too far from here. Some of the others have been drinking it regularly, they quite like it. In fact, I think it's won a few awards of late."

"Well, I shall make my own mind up," Colin said as the finished pint was handed to him. Picking the glass up, he began to inspect the color of the liquid within. "Rather cloudy," he murmured, squinting slightly in order to get a better look, "although I won't know much until it has settled."

"I'll be back in a moment, Colin," the landlord replied, turning and heading back along the bar. "I just have to, uh, check something in the back room."

A few minutes later, while the landlord sat on an upturned crate in the other room and stared at his watch, Colin began to sip at the pint of beer. He took only very small mouthfuls at first, as he began to work his way up to a full gulp.

"Unusual," he said finally, as he once again looked at the glass. He paused, and then he looked along the bar. "Michael, are you back there? I have some thoughts about this ale! Michael! Are you coming? Michael, where are you? I really would like to give you a few notes regarding the way you maintain your kegs!"

Sighing, the landlord put his head in his hands.

***

"And that's really why you'll never get it to the correct temperature while you have oak panels around the bar," Colin observed two hours later, as he set a note down and then got to his feet. "It's the wrong type of wood, you see. I would have thought that you'd know that, Michael, seeing as how you've been in the business for so long."

"I'll have to look into it," the landlord replied wearily as he took the note and set it in the till, and then he retrieved Colin's change and handed it to him. "I'm not sure that I'm in a position to be stripping the entire bar down, though. Not at the moment, not with things the way they are."

"Then you're dooming yourself to poor beer," Colin said, eyeing the change for a moment. "I believe you owe me another five pennies."

"I do?"

The landlord peered at the coins in Colin's palm, and then he sighed.

"Sorry, Colin," he added, turning back to the till. "You know how it is."

"You'll have to get up early to catch me out," Colin replied with a grin. "Those pennies add up. Why, if you took five every time I came in, by the end of the year you'd have fifteen pounds extra off me, maybe more."

"Yes, Colin. I'm sorry, I -"

"And if you did the same to all your other drinkers, well, you'd be swiping enough to pay for a nice little weekend away. I know some people don't notice that sort of thing, but I've always had a very keen eye for sleight of hand."

"As I said, Colin, it was a mistake." He placed a 5p piece in Colin's palm. "It won't happen again."

"I hope it doesn't," Colin replied. "I'll have to mention it to the others, next time I see them in here, and tell them to always check their change. I know what people are like when they're inebriated, they tend to miss these things, and a flashy landlord might take advantage of that fact. Not that I'm accusing you of any such dishonesty, Michael, of course, but one must always be on top of these things, must one not?"

"Yes, Colin," the landlord said, forcing a faint smile.

Stopping at the front door, Colin looked back across the empty room for a moment, and finally he furrowed his brow.

"You know," he continued, "it's odd that I always miss the others these days. I really must make sure that my streak of bad lucks ends soon. I miss the days when I'd come in and find Taff and

Malc and all the others sitting around, ready for a good chinwag. I never see them at all now. I suppose they must be spending the evenings at home with their wives, although I can't imagine that they're very happy about that. They always used to complain about them so much."

"It's a mystery," the landlord agreed.

With that, Colin pulled the door open, revealing the windy, rainy night outside. Waves were crashing against the beach just a few hundred meters away, and Colin stood for a moment and observed the mighty tempest.

"It's on nights like these," he said proudly, "that I'm glad to only live around the corner!"

Finally he stepped out into the storm and let the door swing shut, and the sound of his footsteps could be heard trampling across the pebbles as he made his way around the side of the pub and along the little road that led to a neat row of cottages.

A few seconds later, the pub's back door opened and several rain-soaked faces peered through.

"Phew," Malcolm Lugford said with a sigh, as the landlord began to pour a fresh round, "I thought he was never going to leave."

***

As the storm whipped up and blew nearby trees,

Colin Obford struggled along the pebbly road. The wind was so strong, Colin's coat was almost blown open, and he had to really push against the maelstrom as he fished in his pockets for his keys.

"Home safe at last," he said as he reached his front door and looked up at the cottage's windows. He hesitated, and then a faint smile crossed his lips. "And how, I wonder, is my little friend doing tonight?"

***

The front door shuddered shut with a satisfying click, and Colin took a moment to slide the bolt across before turning and looking across the hallway. He stood completely still for a few seconds, listening to the silence of the house and the sounds of the storm battering the windows, and then his smile grew as he began to remove his coat.

"I'm home, my dear," he announced quite loudly, as he unwound the scarf from around his neck. "There's a gale blowing out there, you might have heard. Nobody else in the pub again tonight. The weather'll be to blame for that, I'd wager."

He hung his coat and scarf on the hook, and then he huffed and puffed as he took a seat and began to remove his shoes.

"I love a good storm," he continued, with a hint of melancholy in his voice. "Sometimes I think they don't make storms the way they used to. When I was a boy, storms were regularly deadly, you'd often hear of a few souls getting lost. Now it seems as if storms, like everything else in this world, have been flattened out and made bland and harmless."

He set his shoes down, and then he paused for a moment in order to delay the moment of rising. His hips were bad, as was his right leg, and he preferred to avoid the pain for a few more seconds.

"I should watch what I wish for, though," he said with a sigh. "One night, a storm might come along and blow these cottages clean away, and then I'll be sorry. One shouldn't tempt fate, should one?"

He took a deep breath, and then he looked up the stairs toward the landing.

"Then again," he added, "you of all people know that, do you not?"

He waited, leaving just enough time for an answer, and then he hauled himself to his feet. Letting out a gasp, he took a moment to steady himself against the banister, and then he shuffled through to the kitchen.

"A good storm should bring out the best in you, I'd think," he muttered. "It's nicely atmospheric. Doesn't that stir your soul? Or whatever's left of your soul, at least." He stopped at the counter and poured himself a beer. "One would think that you'd get into the mood a little and up your game, but I suppose that might be a forlorn hope. After all, your track record is rather -"

Before he could finish, he heard a loud bump from the room above. Looking up at the ceiling, he listened for another bump, but he heard only the sound of the storm outside. The bump, however, had most certainly come from inside the cottage, and this filled him with joy as a smile crept across his lips.

"Is that it?" he asked. "Is that all you've got? Come on, my pretty little thing, if you can't muster something more formidable on a wet and windy night, then there's really not much point to you, is there? I've almost lost faith in you. I'm so nearly ready to accept that you don't have it in you, but why don't you prove me wrong, eh?"

He paused; waiting, listening, hoping.

"For once in your miserable afterlife," he continued, "can't you haunt me properly?"

***

Up in the master bedroom of the little cottage, directly above the kitchen, the ghost of Annabelle Ward stood completely still and tried not to make another noise.

"For once in your miserable afterlife," she heard Colin Obford saying downstairs, "can't you haunt me properly?"

She looked over at the edge of the nightstand. Just a few seconds earlier, she'd bumped into the nightstand and caused a brief but very loud clatter, and this had most certainly attracted Colin's attention. Annabelle had been hoping that the storm would offer blessed relief, at least for a few hours, since she theorized that all the loud noises outside the cottage would disguise any sounds she caused on the inside. She hadn't fully taken her own clumsiness into account, however, and she was starting to realize that she was in for yet another evening of Colin's mocking tone.

Wincing, she heard a floorboard creak downstairs, which she knew meant that Colin was heading through to the hallway.

"Do you hear me up there?" he roared. "I expect fireworks tonight!"

She waited, but now he'd fallen silent. Was he making his way up to the landing? She'd not heard any creaking sounds coming from the stairs, but she knew that Colin could be very crafty when he was so inclined. Even at that moment, she imagined him picking his way up the stairs, avoiding all the loose sections, and she felt a sense of absolute dread filling her chest. In her short life, and in her century of death too, Annabelle Ward had never felt as much anxiety as she felt when Colin was at home.

Still, as the minutes passed, she began to

hold out hope that he remained downstairs. She knew she'd have to find out for certain, however, so she finally crept across the bedroom and peered out to take a look at the landing.

Nothing.

She allowed herself a quiet sigh of relief, even though she knew that the evening had really only just begun.

Right on cue, she heard the sofa creaking downstairs, which could only mean that Colin had settled himself down to watch a film. That would at least give her an hour and a half of peace, and sure enough a moment later she heard the television being switched on. Televisions hadn't been around when she was alive, but during her time as a ghost she'd gradually grown accustomed to all the new developments in the land of the living, and she was particularly grateful for televisions. Any time Colin Obford settled down to watch a film, Annabelle knew that she'd be safe for a little while.

And that would give her time to hide.

***

"What a load of tosh," Colin grumbled as the film's end credits began to roll. "That's ninety minutes of my life that I'll never get back."

He switched the television off and tossed the remote control onto the empty side of the sofa, and then he glanced up at the ceiling. The film had been a noisy old war drama filled with explosions and shouting voices, so he supposed that he might not necessarily have heard any bumps of creaks coming from upstairs. Now, as he listened for some hint of the ghost's presence, he couldn't help but feel rather disappointed.

Wincing with pain, he rose from the sofa and shuffled over to the desk, where his latest research papers lay set out. Ever since he'd purchased the cottage, a little over a year earlier, he'd been painstakingly researching the history not only of the property itself but of the entire town, and in recent months he'd rather hit the jackpot. His shaking hands fumbled for a moment as he tried to find his latest findings, and finally he held up one of the tattered old photos he'd obtained from the local library.

The photo showed a young woman, smiling and happy as she stood outside the cottage with an older man. Turning the photo over, Colin once again read the handwritten note.

"Mr. Charles Ward," he said out loud, "and..."

He once again looked to the ceiling, and then he raised his voice.

"Ms. Annabelle Ward, his daughter."

He waited in case the mention of that name might bring about a recriminatory bump or two, and then he set the photo down and wandered over to the doorway. Looking up at the stairs, he felt a great sense of satisfaction at the realization that he was now closer than ever to understanding the nature of the cottage's haunting. Thanks to several websites, as well as some good old-fashioned detective work locally, he'd managed to build up a fairly strong account of the life of the Wards, and particularly the life and tragic early death of young Annabelle.

"I say," he called out, "would you like to come downstairs for a chat? You're not very good at haunting me, but you might at least help with my research."

He waited.

Silence, as usual.

"I know your name," he continued. "You're Annabelle Ward, and you died at the tender age of nineteen. You were hit by a horse and cart right outside this very cottage. You weren't killed instantly. Rather, you lingered for several days in bed, in the room that is now my own. By all accounts your injuries were severe, and your father's efforts to keep you alive were considered most cruel by many in the area. It's said that there was general relief when you died, and there were rumors that your father had finally relented and had placed a pillow over your face."

Again, he waited.

"Come on," he muttered under his breath,

"at least have the guts to give me a good scare. Your death was rather unfortunate, and I suppose that should be enough to give you a chip on your shoulder."

Stepping forward, he approached the foot of the stairs and stopped once more to listen. He'd been trying to goad the ghost for several nights, without success.

"What is it that keeps you here?" he called out. "Is it the pain of your death? Is it the fact that your own father ended your life? Or do you consider yourself to have unfinished business? There must be a reason, Ms. Ward, so don't be shy. Let's have it!"

When this attempt failed, Colin paused for a few seconds before starting to make his way up the stairs.

"I'm starting to lose my patience," he announced. "If you insist on lingering in my home, young lady, then the least you can do is answer my questions!"

***

Hiding in the wardrobe in the spare room, crouching at the bottom, Annabelle listened to the sound of Colin's footsteps reaching the top of the stairs.

Please, she thought to herself, *just leave me*

alone.

"I know you're up here somewhere," Colin said on the landing. "You much prefer being upstairs, do you not? I wonder why that is. Now, how about we try to improve the atmosphere a little?"

A moment later, the lights clicked off, and Annabella realized that Colin was in a particularly confrontational mood. He'd been pestering her for a while, ever since she's inadvertently allowed herself to be seen one night. Up until then, she'd managed to mostly stay quiet save for a few clumsy bumps. Once she'd been seen, however, everything had changed and Colin had been determined to draw her out into the light.

Annabelle, on the other hand, just wanted to be left alone. She had no desire to actively haunt anybody. Indeed, she didn't even understand why she had stayed in the cottage at all.

"Are you in here, my dear?" Colin asked, as he made his way into the other bedroom and gently pushed the door open. "There's no need to be scared, you know."

Forcing herself to be brave, Annabelle leaned forward and peered out through the tiny gap in the wardrobe's doors. She couldn't see Colin, but as she looked across the darkened bedroom she realized that she was going to have to find somewhere else to hide. She wasn't sure why, but she found it very difficult to keep from being seen, and she had yet to understand quite why she was sometimes visible and sometimes invisible. That was just one of the many ways in which she worried she was inadequate as a ghost, perhaps even a little unintelligent.

"Do you remember your own death?" Colin called out. "I've read that sometimes the dead do not recall their final moments. Do you remember the weight of the horse and cart as they fell upon you?"

She did.

Feeling a shudder pass through her body, Annabelle tried not to think back to that awful moment. In her mind's eye, she could already see the whinnying black horse bearing down on her, and she could feel the road thundering beneath her feet. She could hear the cries of onlookers, too, and a moment later she remembered the sensation of being knocked to the ground and of then having the horse's front leg slam down against one side of her face, shattering her cheekbone and jaw. The pain had been so stark, so intense, and she'd felt blood burst into her mouth. One eye had been destroyed in the impact, too, and she recalled her own desperate attempts to stand.

Poor Robin.

Annabelle had been on her way to meet Robin that day, and she sometimes wondered whether the accident had been the Lord's way of intervening and keeping them apart. Certainly, Robin had visited her during her lingering final days in bed, but he'd attended out of duty rather than love and she'd been vaguely aware of his discomfort. Eventually he'd stopped visiting entirely, which was when Annabelle had come to understand that he hadn't loved her, not truly. She'd longed for death, and then one night her father had entered the room and picked up a pillow.

She wasn't sure what had happened after that, or at least she did not remember the end. She'd managed to put it out of her mind, at least until Colin had started reminding her every night.

"If it's revenge you seek, the architects of your demise are long gone," Colin said, and suddenly he was in the room.

Annabelle pulled back, terrified that the wardrobe might be opened at any moment, unable to predict whether she would or would not be visible.

A floorboard creaked in the middle of the room, and then another.

Colin was edging closer.

"It must be so lonely, haunting this little cottage," he continued. "What do you get out of it, anyway? Sometimes days go by and I never see or hear any hint of you. Then there are days when you seem much more present. I've read about hauntings, and it seems highly unusual for a ghost to act the way that you do. I have to wonder, therefore... what makes you different?"

Pulling back further into the darkness of the wardrobe, Annabelle kept her gaze fixed on the door. She heard another floorboard creaking, this one even closer than the last, and then silence fell.

She waited.

Colin said nothing.

Was he gone? Although she desperately hoped that he had given up for the night, Annabelle could not quite believe that she was yet in the clear. She continued to stare at the crack in the door, but as the minutes ticked past she began to feel a flicker of hope as she realized that perhaps – for whatever reason – Colin had grown tired and had made his way through to the master bedroom. She craned her neck, peering through the crack and searching for any sign of her tormentor, but now the cottage was entirely quiet and she was even tempted to wonder whether Colin might have gone back out to the pub.

Finally, after a few more minutes, she realized that she couldn't spend the entire night cooped up in the wardrobe.

Leaning forward, she immediately flinched as she felt the wardrobe shift slightly beneath her, accompanied by a faint creaking sound. She waited in case Colin took this cue to strike, and then she reached out and told herself that she had no choice: she would have to open the wardrobe doors and climb out.

She took a deep breath, which was more of a habit than a necessity, and then she very slowly began to push one of the doors open. The hinges creaked, of course, but gradually Annabelle was able to see all the way across the dark, empty second bedroom. She swallowed hard – another habit – before pushing the door fully open, and it was at that moment that she realized her heart would have been beating furiously if she'd possessed a heart at all.

She looked around.

Nothing.

Colin seemed to have vanished into thin air.

For a few second, Annabelle wondered whether she might have drifted off into a brief period of unconsciousness. That happened occasionally, although not usually when she was in such a heightened state of fear. She found it hard to believe that Colin could have crept away without making a sound, however, so she resolved to simply clamber out of the wardrobe and find somewhere safer to hide for the rest of the night.

The door creaked again as she began to clamber to her feet. Once she was out, she took a moment to listen once more to the silent house, and then she turned to shut the wardrobe.

"Boo!" Colin said with a huge grin, having been hiding behind the open door.

Screaming, Annabelle turned and ran from the room.

***

"I rather feel," Colin said a few seconds later, as he stepped out onto the landing, "that *I'm* the one who should be racing around in a state of panic. After all, I'm the one's who's alive, and you're the..."

His voice trailed off for a moment as he saw that the door downstairs, leading into the front room, was swinging slightly. As if it had been bumped.

"You're the ghost," he added under his breath, before setting off down the stairs.

By the time he got down into the hallway, Colin was feeling a little tired. His knees were giving him gyp, and he had to stop for a moment to pull himself together. Looking into the front room, he saw no sign of Annabelle Ward, but he was quite certain that she had made one of her rare excursions down to the ground floor of the cottage. For some reason, she tended usually to remain in the upper rooms.

"I have some more notes that you might find useful," he said finally, as he shuffled through to the front room and looked around for some sign of Annabelle. "I hope that this time you'll actually pay attention, because your haunting so far has been –

for lack of a better word – woefully inadequate. You haven't once raised my pulse. You haven't scared me at all."

Realizing that Annabelle had hidden herself away, he made his way over to his favorite armchair and took a seat.

"Now," he continued, "the first thing is the element of surprise. I knew you were in that wardrobe from the moment I got upstairs. I humored you, I gave you time to come up with some other ruse, and you really should have used that time."

Spotting some biscuit crumbs on the table next to the armchair, he reached over and gathered them into the palm of his hand, and then he poured them into his mouth.

"Second," he said, "you must be more proactive. Scream at me, lunge at me, just do *something* that actually makes an impression. I don't know if you're capable of manifesting yourself in some other manner, but perhaps consider showing me your features as they were at the moment of death. I imagine your face was truly horrific, so why not give me a scare by letting me see?"

He licked a few more crumbs from his hand, and then he paused for a moment as he pondered his next sliver of advice.

"Third," he added with a calculated sigh, "you could try using a few more props. How about leaving a message, written on the wall in blood? Or how about just throwing a few things at me? Lord knows, I have a lot of junk in this place, so why not send a plate or two crashing toward my head? That would at least keep me on my toes."

He sniffed, and then he stuck a fingertip into his right nostril, attending to an itch.

"Are you after revenge?" he asked. "That's something else that's missing here. You show no purpose, no sense of being here for a particular reason. Are you grief-stricken? Do you refuse to accept that you're dead? Are you after revenge? At the moment, you just seem to hang around in a rather limp manner. You must be lonely, so why not occupy yourself with a little project?"

He waited.

Silence.

"To be honest," he said finally, "I know this might upset you, but I rather doubt that you've got what it takes to be a good ghost. When I purchased this cottage, the previous owners mentioned that they'd heard a few odd bumps in the night, and that they'd perhaps made contact with a spirit during a séance evening. I'm minded to think that if you were going to be an effective ghost, you'd have managed it by now and -"

Stopping suddenly, he spotted a hint of movement reflected in one of the windows of the dresser. Sure enough, he saw the pale, ghostly face of Annabelle Ward staring back at him, and he immediately turned to look over his shoulder. Spotting nothing, however, he turned back to the dresser, only to find that the face was no longer visible.

"Is that *it*?" he asked, before chuckling merrily. "Was that brief appearance supposed to scare me? My dear, that wouldn't have scared a choir boy, I'm afraid. You really don't have it in you, do you? You're just not a very good ghost. I suppose not everyone can be good at everything, but you could at least try harder."

Leaning back in the chair, he tried to get comfortable, but then he heard a floorboard creaking in the hallway and he immediately got to his feet, just in time to spot a shadow moving through into the kitchen.

"Aha!" he cried out, setting off after her. "The game is once more afoot!"

Filled with a renewed sense of zeal, he hurried to the kitchen just as he heard the sound of glass smashing. Reaching the doorway, he saw that a cup had been knocked from the sideboard.

"Is that it?" he asked, his voice filled with a sense of disappointment. "Well done, my dear, you broke a cup. How terrifying."

Sighing again, he wandered over and crouched down to pick up the pieces.

"I suppose you might score marks for being

irritating," he continued, "but that's hardly high praise for a ghost, is it?" Wincing as he felt a sharp pain in his back, he paused for a moment before getting to his feet, and he had to steady himself against the side of the counter. "Do I need to invest in some new cups," he added, "just so that you can knock them over? If that's the best you can come up with, then I rather think that there's no point. You've been dead for a hundred years, girl. Hasn't that been enough time for you to think up something new?"

He turned to head back to the door.

Suddenly Annabelle stepped toward him and screamed. Her pale face, filled with fury, was contorted into a vision of fury.

Colin stared at her, his expression almost blank save for a very faint smirk.

Annabelle's scream ended, and she found herself staring at the man.

"Is that it?" he asked. "Are you done?"

He waited, but Annabelle seemed frozen in place, as if she couldn't quite believe that her plan had failed. For Colin, the moment was rather amusing, and his smirk grew to become a broad, beaming smile.

"You didn't listen to a word that I said, did you?" he said with another labored sigh. "Anyone who's ever seen even a bottom-of-the-barrel horror film knows that jump scares are rarely effective, especially against a superior mind. Is this your pathetic attempt to scare me? What next, will you throw a cat at me from behind a set of shelves?" He looked her up and down for a moment, and his sense of disappointment was plain to see. "Really, young lady, your lack of creativity is breathtaking. I'm starting to think that you might be a little dense."

She screamed again, but this time she disappeared halfway through, leaving the last of her scream hanging in the air.

"Desperation is never frightening," Colin said confidently. "You really are terribly poor at this haunting malarkey. Let me give you some more pointers. If you want to be a truly successful ghost, you will need to take into account ten clear and steadfast rules that I myself have identified. Wherever you are right now, I'm sure you can hear me, so I shall begin with the first of those rules. Listen very carefully."

***

"It's no good repeating yourself," Colin continued an hour later, warming to the theme of his sixth rule as he carried a glass of wine into the hallway. "I recognize that you have limited means at your disposal here in the cottage, but really you need to be more adaptable. Which brings me onto the seventh rule, in a rather roundabout way."

Stopping for a moment, he listened for any hint of Annabelle's presence.

"I know you can hear me," he told her. "This isn't a very big cottage. I do hope that you're taking notes. You really can learn a lot from me, young lady."

Upstairs, in the corner of the master bedroom, Annabelle sat hunched on the floor with her hands over her ears. She did not understand all the rules of her ghostly life, but she had found that she was unable to ever leave the cottage, which meant that she had limited opportunities to get away from Colin's regular, lengthy speeches. Even putting her hands over her ears was a rather ineffective approach, and she'd been unable to drown out his droning voice.

"What you need is spontaneity," he called out from downstairs. "Do you hear me? Be more spontaneous in your haunting! And that's where my seventh point really comes in, because everybody knows that ghosts must be filled with anger and hatred. You have no choice, do you hear me! You simply *must* hate the living!"

"Shut up," she whispered, as she began to rock back and forth on the floor. "It's after midnight. Why can't you just go to sleep?"

"The hatred must drive you," Colin said, and suddenly his footsteps rang out on the stairs. "It must fill your soul, even at the expense of your rational mind. It's not really that difficult, other ghosts manage it all the time, you just seem to be a little slow on the uptake. I suppose there might be something wrong with you. Tell me, did anybody describe you as thick or stupid while you were alive?"

"Stop," Annabelle whispered, realizing that he was coming closer, "please, I can't take this anymore. Why must I be trapped here with him? Why can't I go into the light? Why can't I join my family, wherever they are?"

"Fortune favors the bold," Colin explained, and now he was reaching the top of the stairs. "You really mustn't be afraid of failure. You must experiment."

Launching herself to her feet, Annabelle marched to the door, determined to find some fresh place to hide. As she was about to go out onto the landing, however, she found herself once again face to face with Colin.

"It's important to remember the rules," he told her calmly. "Only idiots break the rules."

Unable to help herself, Annabelle screamed in his face, and then she stepped straight through him and hurried into the old third bedroom. Stopping, she remembered with a sigh that while the room had been for sleeping when she was alive, it was now a bathroom. She turned to walk out, only to find herself facing Colin yet again.

"That was better," he informed her, "but still not quite up to scratch. I'm not sensing any real yearning for revenge."

Trying to ignore him, she hurried into the second bedroom, before stopping as she realized that the only place to hide was the wardrobe. She'd already tried that, just a few hours earlier, and she was starting to feel as if she'd never be able to get away from Colin Obford. She considered her options for a moment, before turning to find that he was standing just a few feet away.

"Are you able to materialize and de-materialize at will?" he asked. "I feel that would be very useful, and it might enable you to be a little more subtle."

He stepped closer.

"Subtlety isn't exactly your middle name, my dear, is it?"

"Leave me alone!" she replied through gritted teeth.

"That's another error," he told her, as he took his pen and made a note on the pad of paper he was carrying around. "It's actually part of my eighth lesson, so if you don't mind, I'll circle back around to address that point a little later. For now, I'd really like to return to the subject of rules. You see, you seem to be fundamentally lacking when it comes to an understanding of how a ghost should behave. That's not entirely your fault, of course. I rather think that the proliferation of horror films has made many of us living folk rather jaded, and of course you were alive long before such things were part of general pop culture. Not that I'm excusing you, but -"

Before she could hold back, Annabelle screamed again and stormed through to the master bedroom, and then time she slammed the door shut as she went.

"I'm going to lose my mind," she said, as ghostly tears ran down her face. She clenched her fists tight, but even this was no relief. "I'm going to end up as some kind of lunatic."

"I'm just going to fetch a snack!" Colin called out from the landing. "I'll be back up in a moment or two, and then I'll tell you my theory about the changing nature of human fear. It's rather revolutionary, some might even say that it's daring, but I do think it might explain some of your failures. I'll be back in a jiffy!"

"Please don't," Annabelle whispered, as she heard Colin heading to the stairs.

"I think I'm really going to be able to help you!"

"Shut up!" she screamed, putting her hands against either side of her head. "Just shut up! Shut up! Shut up! Shut up!"

"Oh," he added, "and one more thing I -"

Suddenly she heard a terrible cry, followed

by a series of loud thuds that seemed to be moving down the stairs, and then she flinched as something slammed into the floor in the hallway down below.

After a few seconds, Annabelle made her way back across the room. She pulled the door open and leaned out to look at the landing, and then she walked to the top of the stairs and looked down. Gasping, she saw the horrific sight of Colin Obford gasping for air on the floor next to the bottom step. Slowly, the man turned and looked back up at her, and she saw that he must have fallen and landed on his pen, which was embedded in one side of his throat.

Reaching up, Colin grabbed the pen and pulled it out, and blood immediately began to spray from the wound, arching through the air and splattering against the far wall.

"Help me!" Colin cried out, barely able to speak at all.

He tried to get to his feet, but he quickly fell back down and a moment later he rolled onto his side. Clutching his injured neck as blood continued to seep out, he tried to say something else, but blood was running from one corner of his mouth and he was already extremely pale.

Annabelle simply stood at the top of the stairs, listening to the sound of the storm outside and watching as the last trace of life left Colin Obford's body. And then, finally, the cottage silent.

***

"Mummy, I can't find my toothbrush!" Hamish shouted from the bathroom. "I think Louise has hidden it!"

"I haven't hidden anything!" his sister yelled from her bedroom "Mummy, Hamish is making things up again!"

"I am not!" the boy insisted.

"I won't tell the pair of you again," Rachel said, stopping at the foot of the stairs, surrounded by the suitcases she'd just carried in from the car. "If you can't behave, you'll both have to go straight to bed. Is that really how you want to start our holiday?"

"I didn't hide your toothbrush," Louise grumbled. "Why would I do something stupid like that?"

"She didn't hide your toothbrush, young man," Colin said, standing right next to Hamish as he squeezed toothpaste onto his finger and began to clean his teeth without a brush. "I did that, when you weren't looking. Do you feel your mind starting to burn with uncertainty? Do you sense, even now, that I am with you?"

Once he'd finished cleaning his teeth, Hamish spat into the sink and wiped his mouth.

"You might not be able to see me," Colin continued, "but on some deep, subliminal level you sense that I'm here, that your family is not alone in this cottage. This sense is subtle, but it's creeping up on you. Next, you will feel the chill of my touch."

Reaching out, he put a hand on the boy's shoulder. Not reacting at all, Hamish began to floss his teeth.

"Wait for it," Colin said. "I've been practicing this, I know you'll sense me soon. I've been dead for a whole year now, I've had plenty of time to come up with things. I can't tell you how happy I was to learn that the new owners are turning the place into a holiday let. That means fresh victims every week, at least during the warmer months. Now, young man, allow yourself to notice the horror and fear and dread in your heart."

"Mummy!" Hamish called out. "I'm finished! Can I play video games for half an hour before bed?"

"Do you really have to?" Rachel replied from downstairs. "Fine, but thirty minutes maximum, and then I want you to go to sleep! I didn't bring the pair of you all the way down here to the seaside, just for you to spend the entire weekend spending at a screen."

"Yes!" Hamish yelled, as he rushed out of the bathroom.

"Wait!" Colin shouted, shuffling after him.

"You're not paying attention, young man! What's wrong with you children, have you no sense of the world around you? Are you completely oblivious to everything that's happening? I demand that you notice me!"

As he followed Hamish through to the second bedroom, Colin completely ignored the other figure on the landing.

Watching from the shadows, Annabelle barely moved a muscle as Colin continued to rant at the boy. Ever since the holidaymakers had arrived a few hours ago, Annabelle had stood back and waited while Colin had put all his haunting theories into practice. She'd not been particularly surprised to find that Colin had comprehensively failed, although she *was* surprised that the family seemed not to notice him at all. She'd expected some astonishment, perhaps some mockery, but instead Colin seemed completely invisible, as if he was incapable of manifesting himself in any way whatsoever.

Even now, he was gassing himself out and flapping in the second bedroom, and insisting that Hamish should respond to him and show due fear and deference. He had no idea about the strange, little horrors that might prove far more effective.

Finally, slowly, Annabelle took a few steps toward the door. She spotted the new dresser against the far wall, and in the dresser's mirror she saw the reflection of the little girl. Stopping, Annabelle stared at the girl, who was reading a book and trying to ignore the beeps and music from her brother's game console. Colin was still shouting, but Annabelle found that she was able to drown his voice out as she continued to focus her attention on the girl. A few seconds later, she felt a flicker of anticipation in the pit of her stomach as she realized that the girl seemed uncomfortable somehow, as if she could no longer concentrate on her book.

Slowly, Louise looked up, and her reflected face stared directly at Annabelle in the mirror. And then, with no further warning, Louise screamed.

Annabelle stepped back out of view, but Louise was crying out for her mother and pandemonium seemed to have broken out in the bedroom. As Rachel rushed upstairs to see what was wrong, and as Hamish yelled that his sister had soiled the bed, and as Louise screamed about a scary woman, and as Colin shouted at them all to pay attention to his efforts, Annabelle took a deep breath and allowed herself a fine, satisfied smile.

Also by Amy Cross

The Devil, the Witch and the Whore
(The Deal book 1)

"Leave the forest alone. Whatever's out there, just let it be. Don't make it angry."

When a horrific discovery is made at the edge of town, Sheriff James Kopperud realizes the answers he seeks might be waiting beyond in the vast forest. But everybody in the town of Deal knows that there's something out there in the forest, something that should never be disturbed. A deal was made long ago, a deal that was supposed to keep the town safe. And if he insists on investigating the murder of a local girl, James is going to have to break that deal and head out into the wilderness.

Meanwhile, James has no idea that his estranged daughter Ramsey has returned to town. Ramsey is running from something, and she thinks she can find safety in the vast tunnel system that runs beneath the forest. Before long, however, Ramsey finds herself coming face to face with creatures that hide in the shadows. One of these creatures is known as the devil, and another is known as the witch. They're both waiting for the whore to arrive, but for very different reasons. Soon, Ramsey is offered a terrible deal that could save or destroy the entire town, and maybe even the world.

Also by Amy Cross

The Soul Auction

"I saw a woman on the beach. I watched her face a demon."

Thirty years after her mother's death, Alice Ashcroft is drawn back to the coastal English town of Curridge. Somebody in Curridge has been reviewing Alice's novels online, and in those reviews there have been tantalizing hints at a hidden truth. A truth that seems to be linked to her dead mother.

"Thirty years ago, there was a soul auction."

Once she reaches Curridge, Alice finds strange things happening all around her. Something attacks her car. A figure watches her on the beach at night. And when she tries to find the person who has been reviewing her books, she makes a horrific discovery.

What really happened to Alice's mother thirty years ago? Who was she talking to, just moments before dropping dead on the beach? What caused a huge rockfall that nearly tore a nearby cliff-face in half? And what sinister presence is lurking in the grounds of the local church?

Also by Amy Cross

Darper Danver: The Complete First Series

Five years ago, three friends went to a remote cabin in the woods and tried to contact the spirit of a long-dead soldier. They thought they could control whatever happened next. They were wrong...

Newly released from prison, Cassie Briggs returns to Fort Powell, determined to get her life back on track. Soon, however, she begins to suspect that an ancient evil still lurks in the nearby cabin. Was the mysterious Darper Danver really destroyed all those years ago, or does her spirit still linger, waiting for a chance to return?

As Cassie and her ex-boyfriend Fisher are finally forced to face the truth about what happened in the cabin, they realize that Darper isn't ready to let go of their lives just yet. Meanwhile, a vengeful woman plots revenge for her brother's murder, and a New York ghost writer arrives in town to uncover the truth. Before long, strange carvings begin to appear around town and blood starts to flow once again.

Also by Amy Cross

The Ghost of Molly Holt

"Molly Holt is dead. There's nothing to fear in this house."

When three teenagers set out to explore an abandoned house in the middle of a forest, they think they've found the location where the infamous Molly Holt video was filmed.

They've found much more than that...

Tim doesn't believe in ghosts, but he has a crush on a girl who does. That's why he ends up taking her out to the house, and it's also why he lets her take his only flashlight. But as they explore the house together, Tim and Becky start to realize that something else might be lurking in the shadows.

Something that, ten years ago, suffered unimaginable pain.

Something that won't rest until a terrible wrong has been put right.

Also by Amy Cross

American Coven

He kidnapped three women and held them in his basement. He thought they couldn't fight back. He was wrong...

Snatched from the street near her home, Holly Carter is taken to a rural house and thrown down into a stone basement. She meets two other women who have also been kidnapped, and soon Holly learns about the horrific rituals that take place in the house. Eventually, she's called upstairs to take her place in the ice bath.

As her nightmare continues, however, Holly learns about a mysterious power that exists in the basement, and which the three women might be able to harness. When they finally manage to get through the metal door, however, the women have no idea that their fight for freedom is going to stretch out for more than a decade, or that it will culminate in a final, devastating demonstration of their new-found powers.

Also by Amy Cross

The Ash House

Why would anyone ever return to a haunted house?

For Diane Mercer the answer is simple. She's dying of cancer, and she wants to know once and for all whether ghosts are real.

Heading home with her young son, Diane is determined to find out whether the stories are real. After all, everyone else claimed to see and hear strange things in the house over the years. Everyone except Diane had some kind of experience in the house, or in the little ash house in the yard.

As Diane explores the house where she grew up, however, her son is exploring the yard and the forest. And while his mother might be struggling to come to terms with her own impending death, Daniel Mercer is puzzled by fleeting appearances of a strange little girl who seems drawn to the ash house, and by strange, rasping coughs that he keeps hearing at night.

The Ash House is a horror novel about a woman who desperately wants to know what will happen to her when she dies, and about a boy who uncovers the shocking truth about a young girl's murder.

AMY CROSS

AMY CROSS

AMY CROSS

AMY CROSS

AMY CROSS

BOOKS BY AMY CROSS

1. Dark Season: The Complete First Series (2011)
2. Werewolves of Soho (Lupine Howl book 1) (2012)
3. Werewolves of the Other London (Lupine Howl book 2) (2012)
4. Ghosts: The Complete Series (2012)
5. Dark Season: The Complete Second Series (2012)
6. The Children of Black Annis (Lupine Howl book 3) (2012)
7. Destiny of the Last Wolf (Lupine Howl book 4) (2012)
8. Asylum (The Asylum Trilogy book 1) (2012)
9. Dark Season: The Complete Third Series (2013)
10. Devil's Briar (2013)
11. Broken Blue (The Broken Trilogy book 1) (2013)
12. The Night Girl (2013)
13. Days 1 to 4 (Mass Extinction Event book 1) (2013)
14. Days 5 to 8 (Mass Extinction Event book 2) (2013)
15. The Library (The Library Chronicles book 1) (2013)
16. American Coven (2013)
17. Werewolves of Sangreth (Lupine Howl book 5) (2013)
18. Broken White (The Broken Trilogy book 2) (2013)
19. Grave Girl (Grave Girl book 1) (2013)
20. Other People's Bodies (2013)
21. The Shades (2013)
22. The Vampire's Grave and Other Stories (2013)
23. Darper Danver: The Complete First Series (2013)
24. The Hollow Church (2013)
25. The Dead and the Dying (2013)
26. Days 9 to 16 (Mass Extinction Event book 3) (2013)
27. The Girl Who Never Came Back (2013)
28. Ward Z (The Ward Z Series book 1) (2013)
29. Journey to the Library (The Library Chronicles book 2) (2014)
30. The Vampires of Tor Cliff Asylum (2014)
31. The Family Man (2014)
32. The Devil's Blade (2014)
33. The Immortal Wolf (Lupine Howl book 6) (2014)
34. The Dying Streets (Detective Laura Foster book 1) (2014)
35. The Stars My Home (2014)
36. The Ghost in the Rain and Other Stories (2014)
37. Ghosts of the River Thames (The Robinson Chronicles book 1) (2014)
38. The Wolves of Cur'eath (2014)
39. Days 46 to 53 (Mass Extinction Event book 4) (2014)
40. The Man Who Saw the Face of the World (2014)

41. The Art of Dying (Detective Laura Foster book 2) (2014)
42. Raven Revivals (Grave Girl book 2) (2014)
43. Arrival on Thaxos (Dead Souls book 1) (2014)
44. Birthright (Dead Souls book 2) (2014)
45. A Man of Ghosts (Dead Souls book 3) (2014)
46. The Haunting of Hardstone Jail (2014)
47. A Very Respectable Woman (2015)
48. Better the Devil (2015)
49. The Haunting of Marshall Heights (2015)
50. Terror at Camp Everbee (The Ward Z Series book 2) (2015)
51. Guided by Evil (Dead Souls book 4) (2015)
52. Child of a Bloodied Hand (Dead Souls book 5) (2015)
53. Promises of the Dead (Dead Souls book 6) (2015)
54. Days 54 to 61 (Mass Extinction Event book 5) (2015)
55. Angels in the Machine (The Robinson Chronicles book 2) (2015)
56. The Curse of Ah-Qal's Tomb (2015)
57. Broken Red (The Broken Trilogy book 3) (2015)
58. The Farm (2015)
59. Fallen Heroes (Detective Laura Foster book 3) (2015)
60. The Haunting of Emily Stone (2015)
61. Cursed Across Time (Dead Souls book 7) (2015)
62. Destiny of the Dead (Dead Souls book 8) (2015)
63. The Death of Jennifer Kazakos (Dead Souls book 9) (2015)
64. Alice Isn't Well (Death Herself book 1) (2015)
65. Annie's Room (2015)
66. The House on Everley Street (Death Herself book 2) (2015)
67. Meds (The Asylum Trilogy book 2) (2015)
68. Take Me to Church (2015)
69. Ascension (Demon's Grail book 1) (2015)
70. The Priest Hole (Nykolas Freeman book 1) (2015)
71. Eli's Town (2015)
72. The Horror of Raven's Briar Orphanage (Dead Souls book 10) (2015)
73. The Witch of Thaxos (Dead Souls book 11) (2015)
74. The Rise of Ashalla (Dead Souls book 12) (2015)
75. Evolution (Demon's Grail book 2) (2015)
76. The Island (The Island book 1) (2015)
77. The Lighthouse (2015)
78. The Cabin (The Cabin Trilogy book 1) (2015)
79. At the Edge of the Forest (2015)
80. The Devil's Hand (2015)
81. The 13th Demon (Demon's Grail book 3) (2016)
82. After the Cabin (The Cabin Trilogy book 2) (2016)
83. The Border: The Complete Series (2016)
84. The Dead Ones (Death Herself book 3) (2016)

85. A House in London (2016)
86. Persona (The Island book 2) (2016)
87. Battlefield (Nykolas Freeman book 2) (2016)
88. Perfect Little Monsters and Other Stories (2016)
89. The Ghost of Shapley Hall (2016)
90. The Blood House (2016)
91. The Death of Addie Gray (2016)
92. The Girl With Crooked Fangs (2016)
93. Last Wrong Turn (2016)
94. The Body at Auercliff (2016)
95. The Printer From Hell (2016)
96. The Dog (2016)
97. The Nurse (2016)
98. The Haunting of Blackwych Grange (2016)
99. Twisted Little Things and Other Stories (2016)
100. The Horror of Devil's Root Lake (2016)
101. The Disappearance of Katie Wren (2016)
102. B&B (2016)
103. The Bride of Ashbyrn House (2016)
104. The Devil, the Witch and the Whore (The Deal Trilogy book 1) (2016)
105. The Ghosts of Lakeforth Hotel (2016)
106. The Ghost of Longthorn Manor and Other Stories (2016)
107. Laura (2017)
108. The Murder at Skellin Cottage (Jo Mason book 1) (2017)
109. The Curse of Wetherley House (2017)
110. The Ghosts of Hexley Airport (2017)
111. The Return of Rachel Stone (Jo Mason book 2) (2017)
112. Haunted (2017)
113. The Vampire of Downing Street and Other Stories (2017)
114. The Ash House (2017)
115. The Ghost of Molly Holt (2017)
116. The Camera Man (2017)
117. The Soul Auction (2017)
118. The Abyss (The Island book 3) (2017)
119. Broken Window (The House of Jack the Ripper book 1) (2017)
120. In Darkness Dwell (The House of Jack the Ripper book 2) (2017)
121. Cradle to Grave (The House of Jack the Ripper book 3) (2017)
122. The Lady Screams (The House of Jack the Ripper book 4) (2017)
123. A Beast Well Tamed (The House of Jack the Ripper book 5) (2017)
124. Doctor Charles Grazier (The House of Jack the Ripper book 6) (2017)
125. The Raven Watcher (The House of Jack the Ripper book 7) (2017)
126. The Final Act (The House of Jack the Ripper book 8) (2017)
127. Stephen (2017)
128. The Spider (2017)

129. The Mermaid's Revenge (2017)
130. The Girl Who Threw Rocks at the Devil (2018)
131. Friend From the Internet (2018)
132. Beautiful Familiar (2018)
133. One Night at a Soul Auction (2018)
134. 16 Frames of the Devil's Face (2018)
135. The Haunting of Caldgrave House (2018)
136. Like Stones on a Crow's Back (The Deal Trilogy book 2) (2018)
137. Room 9 and Other Stories (2018)
138. The Gravest Girl of All (Grave Girl book 3) (2018)
139. Return to Thaxos (Dead Souls book 13) (2018)
140. The Madness of Annie Radford (The Asylum Trilogy book 3) (2018)
141. The Haunting of Briarwych Church (Briarwych book 1) (2018)
142. I Just Want You To Be Happy (2018)
143. Day 100 (Mass Extinction Event book 6) (2018)
144. The Horror of Briarwych Church (Briarwych book 2) (2018)
145. The Ghost of Briarwych Church (Briarwych book 3) (2018)
146. Lights Out (2019)
147. Apocalypse (The Ward Z Series book 3) (2019)
148. Days 101 to 108 (Mass Extinction Event book 7) (2019)
149. The Haunting of Daniel Bayliss (2019)
150. The Purchase (2019)
151. Harper's Hotel Ghost Girl (Death Herself book 4) (2019)
152. The Haunting of Aldburn House (2019)
153. Days 109 to 116 (Mass Extinction Event book 8) (2019)
154. Bad News (2019)
155. The Wedding of Rachel Blaine (2019)
156. Dark Little Wonders and Other Stories (2019)
157. The Music Man (2019)
158. The Vampire Falls (Three Nights of the Vampire book 1) (2019)
159. The Other Ann (2019)
160. The Butcher's Husband and Other Stories (2019)
161. The Haunting of Lannister Hall (2019)
162. The Vampire Burns (Three Nights of the Vampire book 2) (2019)
163. Days 195 to 202 (Mass Extinction Event book 9) (2019)
164. Escape From Hotel Necro (2019)
165. The Vampire Rises (Three Nights of the Vampire book 3) (2019)
166. Ten Chimes to Midnight: A Collection of Ghost Stories (2019)
167. The Strangler's Daughter (2019)
168. The Beast on the Tracks (2019)
169. The Haunting of the King's Head (2019)
170. I Married a Serial Killer (2019)
171. Your Inhuman Heart (2020)
172. Days 203 to 210 (Mass Extinction Event book 10) (2020)

AMY CROSS

For more information, visit:

www.blackwychbooks.com

AMY CROSS